THE **MILITARY EXECUTION** SAGA

CRANIUM INTEL

GATEWAY 2020

BY

AENEAS MIDDLETON

THE **MILITARY EXECUTION** SAGA

Royal Middleton publishing
New York, NY
royalmiddletonpublishing@gmail.com

ISBN-13: 978-0615637594
ISBN-10: 0615637590

Library of Congress Control Number: 2012907733

Middleton, Aeneas, 1980-
Cranium Intel: Gateway 2020: by Aeneas Middleton –
The Military Execution Saga | 1st Edition | Series 1
Book One (Bk. 1)

Printed in the United States of America

1   2   3   4   5   6   7   8   9   10   11

Cover and book design by Aeneas Middleton

DOCUMENTED FILE# 00003

[COMMANDER AND CHIEF EYES ONLY]

DOCUMENTED FILE# 00004

DEPARTMENT OF DEFENSE

UNITED STATES IN AMERICA

CODE 2020_ 6 87798434 31180

REGISTRATION NUMBER U.S. GOVERNMENT

FILE NUMBER 5573928-2020

DOCUMENTED FILE# 00005

Date: December 24, 3040 AD
To: President Scott Collins

From: Adam Steinberg,
Secretary of Defense

Subject: Cranium Intel

The documents you are about to read are regarding an incident from 2020 A.D. regarding Planet X, involving Cranium Intel technology from the former Portal X Facility in St. Louis, Missouri. They used a stereoscopic vision/neurocranium implant for video/audio recording feeding information which was feedback to their systems in active real-time. This technology was demolished after the Portal X Facility was shut down in St. Louis City following the disappearance of the 46th President.

Recently, the Pentagon has received Intel to our base which was printed out to our systems almost a thousand years later to our present time. This Cranium Intel is formatted with shot angles, including day, night and locations was part of some new hypersonic technology. Digest the information as a reenactment from a director's point of view. The former President's Cranium Intel script technology has recorded exact movements from Micheal W. Logan, a U.S. government military engineer & Portal X Facility scientist.

Mr. President, recently we have received a cranium feed from Micheal Logan's implant. But coming from a young boy in St. Louis City. I have arranged a military team of our best men to look into the matter. Once you have time to digest the Cranium Intel from Mr. Logan, please contact me at your earliest convenience. Some of the Intel from Micheal Logan's cranium had a few transmission problems which is noted in the print feed. Including an well-reoovered audio recording Mr. Logan found himself while he was still alive.

Sincerely,

Adam Steinberg
U.S. Department of Defense
10701 Lambert International Bl, St. Louis, MO - 3040 AD

NEUROCRANIUM IMPLANT
ANALYSIS
INTEL
PROCESSING
CHIP
STEREOSCOPIC IMPLANT
AUDIO
SONIC
IMPLANT
MICHEAL L GAN
E PLURIBUS UNUM
Planet->X<
4745UNITEDSTATESOFAMERICA2020

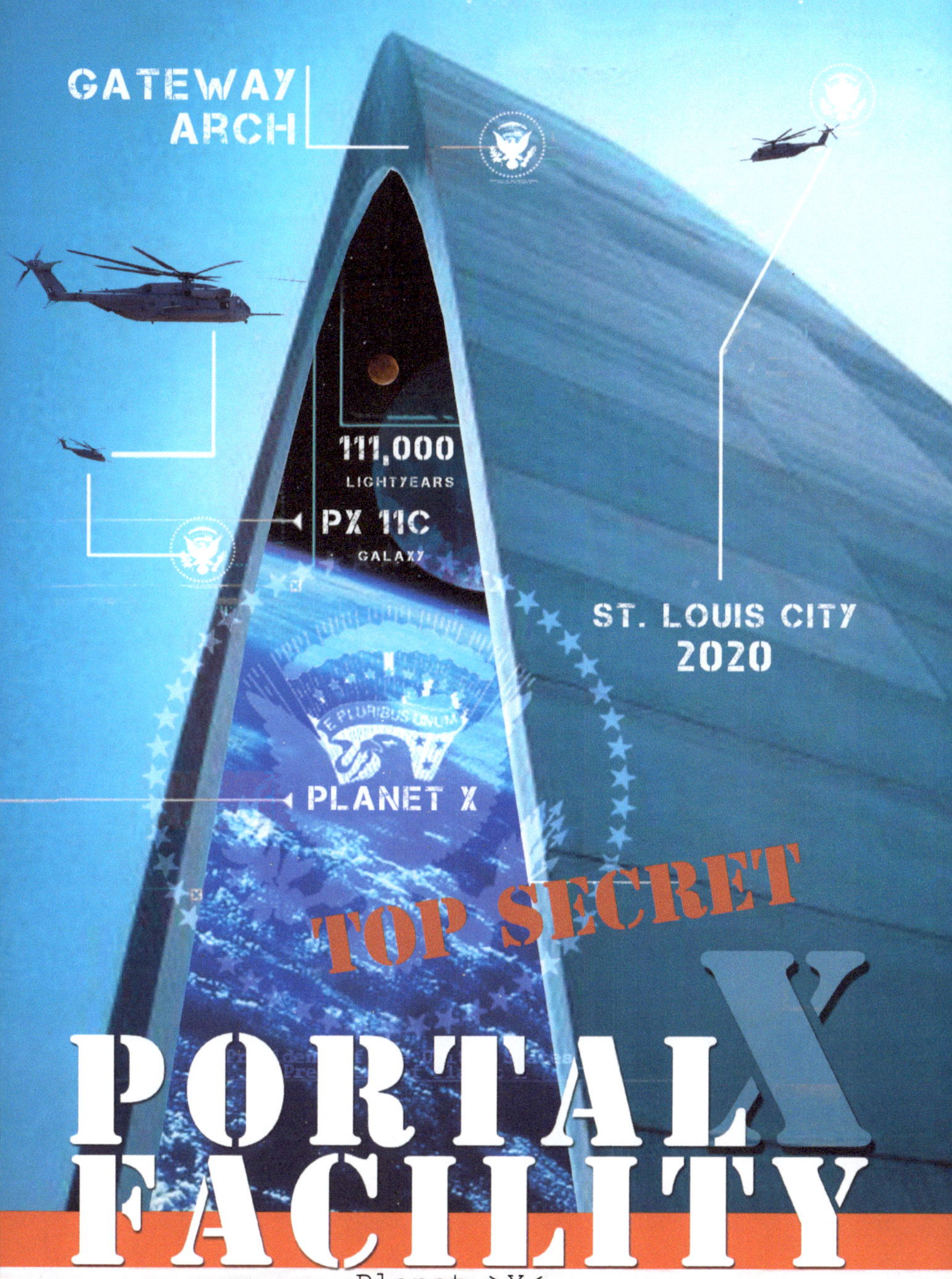

GATEWAY
ARCH
111,000
LIGHTYEARS
PX 11C
GALAXY
E PLURIBUS UNUM
PLANET X
ST. LOUIS CITY
2020
TOP SECRET
PORTAL
FACILITY
X
Planet->X<
4745UNITEDSTATESOFAMERICA2020

DOCUMENTED FILE# 00008
[COMMANDER AND CHIEF EYES ONLY]

TOP SECRET

Cranium Intel Subject: Micheal W. Logan

Recorded: 2020 AD

Type File: Mind Analysis Feed

DEBRIEFING DOCUMENT
CRANIUM IMPLANT SCRIPT
TOP-SECRET INTEL #0001

[INTEL-TRANSMISSION FADE IN]

Complete silence in black outer space, darkness, nebula's cover mother earth with their blue auroras. Lightning and thunder strikes, flashing across the earth. The stars glare bright, their shine never ending in the night sky. Some are Super-Earth's in other constellations, some are dim, almost as a pulse of melody coming from the human heart. The moon has parked itself above the clouds in Normandie, St. Louis, Missouri.

The wind begins to pick up as rain fall slowly onto the ground, a cat runs down the sidewalk, crossing the road passing a gas station on the left-hand side of the street. Traffic sounds are faint. The cat continues down the sidewalk, it's eyes sparkling with a yellow color from the street light flickering high on the corner of Lucas and Hunt.

A car coming from the golf country club up the road starts its engine and then drives away. The rain sounds are hitting trash cans, also a rusted bike with wheels turning in a medium pace motion. In the gas station parking lot, a old gas truck door creaking making an eerie sound. The bell outside the front door is banging against the window, a

"Closed" sign due to repair is hanging in the front window of the store. The sound of cars driving down Highway 70, zooming on their way, when all of a sudden a Harley-Davidson International Lone Star truck bust its way to the light pass the gas station, it's air lock sounds as he breaks stop with high quality precision at the red light. The street light quickly turns green and the driver Jacob Freeberg merges over to the right to head downtown on the highway. Jacob is a Jewish man, Italian mother. He has a tattoo of his wife Marlene and his two kids Ashley and Jennifer on his left shoulder. As Jacob turns around the ramp to get on the highway, he quickly spits a huge piece of phlegm out the window. His tail lights

are the last thing anyone on the road or around this particular highway for the next two minutes.

Back at the abandoned gas station, one of the dim lights inside the store begins to flicker on wall. Usually the gas station is pest free, but with hectic construction from burglarism, the owner and his staff hasn't been able to clean the station up on a everyday basis. But most of the gas station is neat even with the construction gears inside, and a few painting tools. Somehow, with luck. A small mouse has snuck his way into gas station. The only reason why the mouse is even in the gas station is because one of the workers keeps it as a pet inside of his truck. But today he was tired

and left his door slightly crack for the mouse to escape, remaining unnoticed by the construction workers throughout the day, the only place in the gas station is the bathroom. This place has taken a beating, somehow, roaches find their way here all the time, baby roaches are falling out of the sink scattering every direction. Water is dripping out of sink slowly. On top of a dirty rag, which is sitting inside of the sink. A man named Micheal W. Logan is sleeping on the floor, he wakes up, unaware if the situation. Wearing a steel shop jacket, Blue shirt and dark blue carpenter pants.

MICHEAL opens his eyes noticing decayed dead rat covered in maggots right in front of his face. Micheal jumps up,

looking around dazed and confused. He sits down on a chair close by and notices a pocket recorder sticking out of his pocket. MICHEAL pulls out the recorder device from his pocket, dropping a metal hypersonic pen on the bathroom floor. Micheal picks up the recorder pressing play while holding the hypersonic pen device in his hand. Micheal walks up to the bathroom sink, placing the recorder on the edge of the sink, knocking off a couple of roaches. He uses his finger to press play on the recording device which has a sequenced clicking sound. Micheal shakes his head while trying to get a good listen to what is on the recorder device.

END TRANSMISSION 04:39:11

DOCUMENTED FILE# 000014

SAVED IMPLANTATION PRINTED SCRIPT INTEL

**PORTAL X FACILITY
TOP-SECRET FIELD AUDIO
PRINTED FEED
[RECORDED FROM
SUBJECT MICHEAL LOGAN
AUDIO INTEL_CAMERA
DATA
WRITTEN LOG]
#0002**

TOP SECRET
[COMMANDER AND CHIEF EYES ONLY]

(Audio Male Voice)

[Distorted Recording]

"The moon has parked itself near The Gateway Arch. I am currently in downtown St. Louis, Missouri. People still litter the streets like they do not care at all.

It makes me sick to my stomach. Sometimes, I have to take medicine to keep my migraines from being to painful.

DOCUMENTED FILE# 000015

I don't understand how people could destroy such a wonderful world that God created. I do not have much time to talk, Therefore, I'm going to get right to the point. The Portal X Facility was built Over one of America's favorite landmarks...The Gateway Arch. Built on December 1st, 1935. The Arch was originally Designed by Finnish-American Architect pioneers,

Eero Saarinen and Engineer

Hannskari Bandel.

Oh yeah, by the way my identification is Micheal William Logan, number 1180. I used to be a military engineer and scientist for the United States Government. But now , there is a bigger problem." MICHEAL looks at the mirror with the recording device clicking off abruptly beeping loudly throughout the room.

The battery light starts flashing red indicating that its low on power. MICHEAL pauses for a moment adjusting the double A batteries, flipping one battery to the other spot for positive and visa versa. for negative. Micheal coughs, loudly, feeling dizzy again and knocks out cold falling on the floor. He begins to have flashbacks about previous events.

END TRANSMISSION [TIME: UNKNOWN)

DOCUMENTED FILE# 000017

PORTAL X FACILITY
TOP-SECRET SCRIPT
FROM SURGICAL CRANIUM
CAMERA WITH AUDIO FEED
[RECORDED FROM
SUBJECT: MICHEAL LOGAN
WRITTEN LOG]
#0002

TOP SECRET

5. EXT. PORTAL X FACILITY - DAY

-COVERGING DOLLY over, officials in suits and Gov't uniforms are walking into the facility from a HIGH WIDE ANGLE. FOLLOW an American Flag, which is being carried, by one of the soldiers walking towards the entrance of the facility. More guards walking into the FRAME standing outside of facility are awaiting The President of the United States to arrive WITH A LOW

PAN-SHOT of them parking near front of the entrance. THE SECRETARY OF DEFENSE is standing firm, adjusting his uniform. Two soldiers walking into the FRAME, right up to the SUV's. CLOSE UP of the guards hands, opening the door for the high. Government officials get out of SUV's.

[Transmission-feed break]

Government Officials:

*James Whitaker.........President of the United States

*Paul Excalibur......Secretary of Defense

(CUT TO:)

DOCUMENTED FILE# 000019

[FLASHBACK]

5. EXT. PORTAL X FACILITY WALKWAY - DAY

-FULL SHOT of **the President of the United States,** As he steps outside of the SUV walking towards THE SECRETARY OF DEFENSE. They begin shaking hands as they walk into the entrance of the Portal X Facility.

(CUT TO:)

[FLASHBACK]

6. INT. PORTAL X FACILITY LOBBY LEVEL - 1

-PANNING UP from the floor, The Official Seal of the Portal X Facility. A REVERSE

ANGLE of The President and The Secretary conversation begins.

SECRETARY OF DEFENSE

"Welcome Mr. President to The Portal X Facility. Scientist and engineer MICHEAL W. Logan, will demonstrating his new discovery using the gateway arch as a pathway to the new world Planet X.

(CUT TO:)

[FLASHBACK]

7. INT. PORTAL X FACILITY LOBBY – LEVEL 1

-CLOSE UP on THE SECRETARY OF DEFENSE firmly griping The President's hand while handing him some documents with

his other hand. MICHEAL Logan walks down from a stairwell coming from the side-passageway standing next to them. FOLLOW them all walking over to the elevator to the Observation Room.

[Transmission-feed break]

MICHEAL

(Smiling, greeting)

"Good day, Mr. President and Welcome"

THE PRESIDENT OF THE UNITED STATES

(Amused)

"Yes, nice to meet you Mr. Logan it looks like you have been on my radar lately. I have already been briefed on your progress here. I will address our

officials with a pre-speech. Then you will show us what you have discovered. Remember, this information is highly classified,whatever you show today will be treated as sensitive material above top secret material For here on in."

MICHEAL

(Confident)

"Yes sir"

(CUT TO:)

[FLASHBACK]

8. INT. PORTAL X FACILITY - OBSERVATION ROOM - LEVEL 5

-CUT FAST ON THE PRESIDENT MANTLE. Officials

start walking into the observation room from the hallway. PANAGLIDE FROM THE SIDE OF THE ROOM while PANNING UP on The President Seal behind the mantle. The President walks into the FRAME, tapping his fingers on the mantle before he speaks. There is a large rectangle window overlooking the Gateway arch inside the facility. The President looks at the window from the mantle a quick glance and begins to speak.

(CUT TO:)

[FLASHBACK]

9. INT. PORTAL X FACILITY - OBSERVATION ROOM - LEVEL 5

DOCUMENTED FILE# 000024

THE PRESIDENT OF THE UNITED STATES

(Speech to officials)

"Ladies and Gentlemen,

We are making

History tonight.

Mr. Logan has successfully

found a new world

for us as human beings

to start over.

We have to vow to

ourselves to make this a

better world. A better place.

This project has been funded

with over 100 Billion Dollars.

Half of that has been given

to The National Expansion

Memorial for ownership

made under Executive Order 7521.

DOCUMENTED FILE# 000025

Mr. Micheal Logan's dream has

become reality. He envisioned

what most would call insane.

There is a new world

in our universe that we

will call our new home.

Some believed, even if

there was another world

like Earth.

It would be out of reach.

Some scientists came close

by discovering Gliese 581c and 581d,

two super earth planets

nearly twenty light years away.

Some scientists say they would

have potential of a habitable zone.

The Von Bloh et al. Team later discovered

The temperature left

DOCUMENTED FILE# 000026

a large margin for error

for stars to support

life on Gliese 581c

Today,on this very day

I rest assure,

we do not have to

look any further.

We have found Planet X,

an exact copy of our

Planet Mother Earth."

-PANNING along the Government officials

sitting down looking on with amazement.

Anticipating what's next. Some of them

have slight disbelief, crossing their arms

in the back row seats.

[Transmission-feed break]

DOCUMENTED FILE# 000027

THE PRESIDENT OF THE UNITED STATES

(Cont'd Speech)

"With the magic of our own eyes

With the power of god and will.

We have constructed a new facility

over the Gateway Arch for control..

This portal will

lead us to the next chapter that

will be remembered down the ages...

"First we watched the Roman Empire

last for over four-hundred years.

Even Mayan and African cultures

still last today

in our societies.

We've watched humankind

on television taking our

first step on the moon by

Neil Armstrong.

DOCUMENTED FILE# 000028

We have gone to Mars,

finding living organisms.

Now let us take out

first step on another planet,

from another galaxy.

I am proud to show you how

we are going to get to

our new second home. Planet X!"

[Transmission-feed break]

-WHIP PANNING, leading towards the window over looking Level 2, PANNING DOWN towards the St. Louis Gateway Arch.

(CUT TO:)

[FLASHBACK]

10. INT. PORTAL X FACILITY - PORTAL X

DOCUMENTED FILE# 000029

AREA - LEVEL 2

-HANDHELD CAMERA.

FOLLOW MICHEAL walking into the tramcar.

As The President and his officials look

down at MICHEAL walking towards the Arch.

PANNING UP, to the Arch as we see the

elevator rising to the observation area

inside the Arch.

(CUT TO:)

[INTEL-TRANSMISSION FADE IN]

[FLASHBACK]

11. INT. GATEWAY ARCH - OBSERVATION AREA

-ANGLE SHOT ABOVE MICHEAL'S RIGHT

SHOULDER,

MICHEAL looks straight ahead inserting

the metal hypersonic pen device into the front console. SEQUENCE OF SHOTS, of much different instrumentation working inside of the observation room, green lights flickering, red lights beep loudly. Computer-like noises and lights start moving where the hypersonic pen was inserted.

(CUT TO:)

[FLASHBACK]

12. INT. PORTAL X FACILITY - OBSERVATION ROOM - LEVEL 5
-CLOSE-UP, on the President leaning over to talk to **THE SECRETARY OF DEFENSE** privately.

[Transmission-feed break]

DOCUMENTED FILE# 000031

THE PRESIDENT OF THE UNITED STATES

(Pondering)

"Where exactly did Micheal

find this hypersonic device"

SECRETARY OF DEFENSE

(Replying)

"He said he found it near the

Mediterranean Sea near the coast

Of Africa but didn't know

what it was at first.

He said when he moved to

the base in St. Louis

for further research.

He took a walk in the

park and decided to

go in the Gateway Arch

for the first time. He said he was

DOCUMENTED FILE# 000032

carrying the metal hypersonic pen

in his bag just coming from work

and noticed while he was in

the tram car, it started to transform

into something more futuristic.

He said a hologram screen popped up,

showing him the direction

to Planet X."

THE PRESIDENT OF THE UNITED STATES

(Amazed)

"Yeah I read that part

in the report,

The cops had to bust

the door down; he was

locked in there for

six hours straight.

Once the cops opened

DOCUMENTED FILE# 000033

the door everything went

back to normal.

By the way, after this is

over I want to talk to

you about a couple of

Other things as well.

What The?"

(CUT TO:)

[FLASHBACK]

13. INT. PORTAL X FACILITY - PORTAL X

AREA - LEVEL 2

-UP ANGLE, the entire Gateway, begins to

transform with light flashing. Sounds of

machines moving side to side. The entire

Arch is beginning to transform looking

more futuristic.

DOCUMENTED FILE# 000034

(CUT TO:)

[FLASHBACK]

14. INT. GATEWAY ARCH - OBSERVATION AREA

MICHEAL

(Whispering to himself)

"Heaven, my new heaven,

let me see you now"

(CUT TO:)

[FLASHBACK]

15. INT. PORTAL X FACILITY - PORTAL X AREA - LEVEL 2

-CRANE SHOT, looking directly at the middle of the portal inside the Arch. It

has a blue color of light sparkling in the middle. WHIP PANNING, showing MICHEAL walking out of the bottom of the Arch, standing right in front of the blue light. His body disappears also sucked right into a Gateway, leaving a trail of light inside the blue light. The sound of his body through the portal is like a sonic sound of some kind. The blue light starts to take shape almost like a projection screen.

(CUT TO:)

[FLASHBACK]

16. INT. PORTAL X FACILITY - OBSERVATION ROOM - LEVEL 5
-TIGHT ON, the crowd of officials standing up with disbelief as they see a dark body

figure take shape and become clear in the middle of the portal.

CLOSE-UP on The President wiping his eyes while noticing a man-like figure staring right back on the projection screen inside the observation room.

(CUT TO:)

[FLASHBACK]

17. INT. OF THE PLANET X FACILITY LEVEL 2

-CLOSE UP ANGLE, behind MICHEAL as he begins to talk to The President and his Officials....

[Transmission-feed break]

DOCUMENTED FILE# 000037

MICHEAL

(Speaking with

a firm tone)

"As you can see, I am alive.

On a Planet X with no pollution,

no sins, no nuclear weapons,

no diseases, just peace.

Mr. President I give you.."

JUMP CUT

18. INT. GAS STATION BATHROOM - NIGHT

-LOW WIDE ANGLE, on MICHEAL waking up

from the flashback, coughing. CLOSE-UP on

him rubbing the back of his head, where

he notices a glow in the dark tattoo

imprint. The letter "E" reflects off his neck onto a broken mirror behind him on. He spits into the sink, walking out of the bathroom into the parking lot.

19. EXT. GAS STATION PARKING - NIGHT

-LOW PANAGLIDE, MICHEAL notices a jingling noise in one of his pockets, his memory is blurred and cannot remember what happened to him exactly. MICHEAL pulls out a pair of car keys and notices that they are for the 1987 Oldsmobile Grand National parked across the street. He walks over to the car, gets in and drives off.

[Transmission-feed break]

DOCUMENTED FILE# 000039

20a. INT. CAR - CUTLASS - NIGHT

-HIGH WIDE AERIAL SHOT, of MICHEAL driving downtown on Highway 70. He gets off on the Broadway exit. CLOSE-UP, MICHEAL driving underneath the highway, parking near The Landing Downtown.

                                    (CUT TO:)

20b. INT. CAR - CUTLASS - NIGHT

-CLOSE UP, on MICHEAL lighting a cigarette while pressing play once more on the Voice Recorder but notices the batteries are completely dead.

DOCUMENTED FILE# 000040

MICHEAL

(Pissed)

"Damn it"

-TIGHT ON, MICHEAL looking at his watch, looking left and notices a police car driving up the street.

(CUT TO:)

21a. EXT. THE LANDING - DOWNTOWN - NIGHT

***Jennifer Lee**..........FEMALE POLICE OFFICER

-RESUME WIDE, on the female cop stopping in the middle of the street near MICHEAL's car noticing the motor still running.

DOCUMENTED FILE# 000041

She starts running his plates on her laptop, Then steps out of her control car walking a few steps to MICHEAL car.

JENNIFER/Female Police Officer

(Suspiciously)

"Excuse me, Sir,

will you please step

out of the car"

-RESUME WIDE FROM THE FRONT OF MICHEAL'S CAR;

MICHEAL "signs", looking up at her.

MICHEAL

(Weakly replying back)

"Did I do something wrong Officer"

DOCUMENTED FILE# 000042

JENNIFER/Female Police Officer

(Still suspicious)

"Someone reported that there was

a suspicious character parked

on the landing after hours.

So once again, Can you please

step outside the car?"

-CLOSE-UP on Jennifer's eyes, noticing

that MICHEAL looks like he is high on

illegal drugs by his red eyes. MICHEAL

starts scratching his head, gripping his

right hand on the steering wheel.

-PANNING ON Jennifer reaching for her pistol

aiming directly at MICHEAL, thinking he's

a troublemaker or Drug Dealer.

DOCUMENTED FILE# 000043

JENNIFER/Female Police Officer

(Screaming)

"Don't make me use

deadly force mister!

Do you have any

drugs in your vehicle?"

-TIGHT ON, MICHEAL sweating hard, Jennifer
moves her hand towards her radio, calling
in for back up almost waiting for MICHEAL
to move or say something the wrong way.

JENNIFER/Female Police Officer

(Shouting)

"I need back up on the

lower east corner of the landing,

a possible 10-14 in progress.

DOCUMENTED FILE# 000044

DISPATCHER

(Radio voice)

"10-4, sending the closest

available unit. Stand-by!"

-WHIP PANNING, Jennifer snaps her head noticing another car driving down the street towards them. MICHEAL knocks the gun out of her hand pushing her down. Jennifer's head catches the corner of her car, knocking her out cold. PAN, on MICHEAL running away up the nearest alley.

BLACKOUT

FADE IN

DOCUMENTED FILE# 000045

21b. EXT. STREETS OF DOWNTOWN ST. LOUIS - NIGHT

-ANGLE-MACRO SHOT, MICHEAL walking down the street noticing a nightclub at the end of the block. He glances right and notices there is black Crown Victoria parking across the street.

(CUT TO:)

22. INT. GOVERNMENT AGENT CAR - DARK

-SEQUENCE OF SHOTS OF THE TWO AGENTS, MICHEAL noticing two people looking right at him sitting inside the car, with two red dots of cigarettes that are glowing inside the car.

(CUT TO:)

23. EXT. STREETS OF DOWNTOWN ST. LOUIS - NIGHT

-TIGHT ON MICHEAL, trying not to look suspicious, he brushes his hair with his right hand, turning around, facing the doorway to the Eye Candy Strip Night Club entrance.

MICHEAL

(Whispering to himself)

"There must be two of them, what do they want with me?"

(CUT TO:)

DOCUMENTED FILE# 000047

24. INT. GOVERNMENT AGENT CAR - DARK

-ANGLE BETWEEN AGENTS IN THE BACK SEAT OF THE CAR, The 2 Government Agents are looking directly at MICHEAL entering the nightclub. -HANDHELD CAMERA, on MICHEAL walking into the Strip Night Club...

TWO UNDERCOVER AGENTS

(Dark, screwed sounding)

"The Target is identified, pursuing for termination"

(CUT TO:)

25. INT. iCANDY STRIP NIGHT CLUB - NIGHT

-FULL SHOT, showing what is going on in the nightclub, men drinking laughing, women sliding down poles. Women sitting on the laps on guys chatting. HANDHELD CAMERA following behind a woman's hips, to another stripper walking into the FRAME, while laughing with her friends slapping hands.

DJ

(Announcing)
"Welcome to iCandy & Cream.
Fellas get your money out,
Its time to show these
women what you got in
those pockets.
We got the hottest eye candy
In town. Even the

DOCUMENTED FILE# 000049

most committed married men

can't resist the bodies

of these particular

hottest...."

"Ladies its time to

Turn it up, it is the hot hour

Let's get it popping in here".

(CUT TO:)

26. INT. iCANDY - STRIP NIGHT CLUB - NIGHT

-PANNING DOWN, Two drunk men sitting down at a table talking about the particular women in the night club.

DOCUMENTED FILE# 000050

**Bishop*..........Drunk Man #1

**Rodney*.........Drunk Man #2

Bishop-Drunk Man #1

Slurred,Drunk)

"A yo Rodney, Look over there man…"

Rodney-Drunk Man #2

(High pitched)

"What, What's up? Bishop what's up?"

Bishop-Drunk Man #1

Perverted sounding)

"Look at body on her,

Oh my god, I think I in love"

DOCUMENTED FILE# 000051

Rodney-Drunk Man #2

(Silly)

"Man, I ain't even know

Chinese girls be packing

like that?"

Bishop-Drunk Man #1

(Sarcastic)

"Shut up stupid. She's Korean

Don't you see the flag tattooed

on her shoulder blade.

Sometimes I worry about you,

that's why you need to take

your ass back to school.

Take a eye class too, haha

Cause you can't see worth a damn

Either, you as blind as a bat"

DOCUMENTED FILE# 000052

(CUT TO:)

26. INT. EYE CANDY - STRIP NIGHT CLUB - CENTER STAGE

DOWN ANGLE SLOWLY PANNING UP, watching the stripper doing her routine on stage. The Stripper flips up the pole, sliding down upside down with her legs gripping the pole.

                    Rodney-Drunk Man #2

                        (Excited)

            "Oh wee, now that's
        what I'm talking about."

[Transmission-feed break]

DOCUMENTED FILE# 000053

Bishop-Drunk Man #1

"Yeah tell me about it..

I heard the owner, flew her

all the way here from South Korea.

She knows Tae Kwon Do too.

At least that's what

the bartender said.

He also said,

She caught somebody tripping

two weeks ago trying to

stalk her after

she got off work.

He said she grabbed

the stalker with her

two legs wrapped around

his neck with no underwear on, and

her poom poom, was right on

his lips and broke his neck.

DOCUMENTED FILE# 000054

He was trying to rape her

outside her house.

She didn't even get arrested,

she got off too.."

Rodney-Drunk Man #2

(Drunken)

"Man, that's a hell of a

way to go out,

She's like that chick

from Rush Hour 3,...Ha-Ha-Ha"

Bishop-Drunk Man #1

(Laughing)

"Yeahhh, man what I wouldn't

do to get a piece of that.."

-TIGHT ON, Rodney can't help it. All of

that talk about the Asian stripper has

DOCUMENTED FILE# 000055

got him drooling badly. Sounding like a
old grumpy old man moaning loudly.

Rodney-Drunk Man #2

Breathing loudly)
"Yo man..All that talk about
shawty, got me feeling hot"

Bishop-Drunk Man #1

"Yo man get your hands
out your pants,
you perverted nut.
Spend some money and
let the women do that"

-WHIP PANNING, on MICHEAL accidentally
bumping into Bishop spilling his drink
all over Rodney's lap. Bishop stands up

DOCUMENTED FILE# 000056

and falls down because he too drunk...

Bishop-Drunk Man #1

(Yelling)

"You damn fool, you spilled

my drink, I got to spend

my bus money now, to buy

another one.

Why I should kick your ass."

(CUT TO:)

27. INT. iCANDY STRIP NIGHT CLUB - EXIT BACK DOOR - NIGHT

-CUT FAST, on MICHEAL noticing the exit and

heads for it, He turns around for a quick

DOCUMENTED FILE# 000057

second to spot the two agents closing on his position. Both Government agents are sliding through the club unnoticed. (They are very sneaky and are very well trained assassins.)

-WHIP PANNING, towards the door, MICHEAL enters the FRAME, follow MICHEAL with a HANDHELD CAMERA, while he busts open the exit door and races down the alley.

MICHEAL

(Breathing fast, talking to himself)
"I got to get out of here,
who in the hell
are these guys following me?"

(CUT TO:)

DOCUMENTED FILE# 000058

27. EXT. ALLEY- EXIT BACK DOOR - NIGHT

-SPLITS-SCREEN, CAMERA 1-ANGLE REVERSE, showing MICHEAL running down the alley, CAMERA 2-LOW WIDE ANGLE, showing the two agents closing in. They pull their guns out and begin shooting, but MICHEAL never hears any shots, all he notices is the damage the bullets are hitting. One of the agents starts whistling for their attack dogs…

(CUT TO:)

28. EXT. ALLEY - NIGHT

-LOW WIDE ANGLE ON, Two evil wolf looking dogs smash through the window on the Crown

Victoria the agents where driving. The dogs begin running towards their location, they are very quick, and almost look like monsters with teeth so sharp they can cut through metal.

MICHEAL begin running pass another alley and notices the ferocious looking dogs running towards his location. MICHEAL jumps and leaps to climb over a brick divider but the 1st dog has already reached MICHEAL & snags his jeans ripping them.

MICHEAL's arm is caught on the top of the brick divider barbwire. The 2nd dog begins to bite into MICHEAL's right shoe.

MICHEAL

(Screaming)

DOCUMENTED FILE# 000060

"Get off me, let me go arrrgh"

(CUT TO:)

29. EXT. ALLEY - NIGHT

-CRANE SHOT, one of the dogs looses his grip and rips the cuff off his jeans. MICHEAL kicks the other dog in the face while he frees himself as the agents are stuck behind the brick divider.

-TIGHT ON ANGLE, both agents pulling up their collars and report the situation to their leading officer SGT. Biller.

One of the agents starts dialing on high tech mobile device.

TWO UNDERCOVER AGENTS

(Dark, screwed sounding)

DOCUMENTED FILE# 000061

"The target got away."

SGT. BILLER

(Speaking reckless)

"I don't care what

you have to do,

who you have to kill.

Terminate the target

Kill him, NOW!

Do you understand me?

That's an order!"

TWO UNDERCOVER AGENTS

(Dark, deep sounding,

replying in unison)

"Yes Sir"

(CUT TO:)

DOCUMENTED FILE# 000062

30. EXT. BROADWAY AND CONVENTION PLAZA - NIGHT

-HANDHELD CAMERA, On MICHEAL reaching the other end of the alley. He comes out to Lucas Ave. He proceeds left on Lucas, then takes a quick right coming down Broadway to the corner of Broadway and Convention Plaza.

MICHEAL notices a whole bunch of people screaming and walking up to Entry 8 Entrance of the Edward Jones Dome.

MICHEAL

(Talking to himself)

"I have to find somewhere

to blend in. I shook them

this time but something is

telling me they'll be back.
I have to find some help,
but for now, I got to
lay low for a while…"

(CUT TO:)

31. EXT. EDWARD JONES DOME|ENTRY 8 - NIGHT

-SEQUENCE OF SHOTS, on MICHEAL heading in the direction of the Edwards Jones Dome approaching the ticket counter. The clerk has the game on inside the booth. MICHEAL looks at the clerk asking for tickets, quickly glances at the television checking the score.

DOCUMENTED FILE# 000064

[Transmission-feed break]

*TIGHT ON THE TV SCREEN, CAST IS REPORTING,

TV ANNOUNCER 1

[Audio Voice]

"The St. Louis Rams are down

by six points versus

the Dallas Cowboys (score 36-30)

with only fifhteen seconds left.

The Rams just

used their last time

out with possession."

(CUT TO:)

32. EXT. EDWARD JONES DOME - TICKET

DOCUMENTED FILE# 000065

COUNTER|ENTRY 8 - NIGHT

MICHEAL

"Can I have one ticket

for the game, Please?"

FEMALE TICKET CLERK

"There's only fifteen seconds

left in the game sir."

33. INT. TICKET COUNTER|ENTRY 8 - NIGHT

-FULL SHOT, on the Ticket clerk noticing

that MICHEAL is really anxious. Thinking

to herself that he just wants to see the

end of the football game.

DOCUMENTED FILE# 000066

FEMALE TICKET CLERK

(Smiling)

"Go ahead. You do not have to pay,
here is your ticket, head up
the stairwell to section 333,
enjoy the game."

**32. EXT. EDWARD JONES DOME - TICKET
COUNTER|ENTRY 8 - NIGHT**

MICHEAL

(Out of breath/anxious)

"Thank you.."

(CUT TO:)

33. INT. EDWARD JONES DOME - NIGHT

DOCUMENTED FILE# 000067

-SEQUENCE OF SHOTS, on MICHEAL walking towards seat section 333 of the Dome. Somehow the two agents have followed him without MICHEAL knowing. They are following him up the stairwell in unison.

(CUT TO:)

34. INT. TV CAST BOOTH|EDWARD JONES DOME - NIGHT

**Terry Roman*..............TV ANNOUNCER 1
**Chris Miller*...........TV ANNOUNCER 2

Terry-TV ANNOUNCER 1

(Excited)

"Welcome back to The Dome,

where the St. Louis Rams are

at home against the Dallas Cowboys.

The Rams called their final timeout

with the ball on their own 30.

Its 4th down and 10, and this will

clearly be the last play of the game

With 15 seconds left.

Let's take you down on the field

with Chris Miller"

(CUT TO:)

**35. INT. SIDELINE|EDWARD JONES DOME -
NIGHT**

-SEQUENCE OF SHOTS, on Chris Miller

standing on the sideline while the players

are running back to the field. The coach is reading his playbook, the crowd is going nuts. Two fat guys with huge bellies are bumping each other's chest, ready for the last play.

Chris-TV ANNOUNCER 2

(Yelling)

"Thanks Terry, the noise level

has increased to the point

where I can barely hear myself.

The hometown fans are expecting

the Rams to go all the

way with this one..

The Rams and Cowboys setting

up their formation..."

(CUT TO:)

DOCUMENTED FILE# 000070

36. INT.   FIELD|EDWARD JONES DOME – NIGHT

-TIGHT ON, the back Rams quarterbacks helmet, SEQUENCE OF SHOTS of The centers fingers turning the football. The lineman sticking their foot into the ground. The Dallas Cowboys, are gripping their fist. The Dallas cowboys' defensive coach is pointing towards the receivers. The Dallas head coach is covering his mouth with his clipboard.

Rams Quarterback

"Set, 1, 2, Set…34,22 Hut"

(CUT TO:)

DOCUMENTED FILE# 000071

**37. INT. SIDELINE|EDWARD JONES DOME -
NIGHT**

> **Chris-TV ANNOUNCER 2**
> (Announcing Cont'd)
> "The quarterback jumps back,
> the wide receivers sprint
> out going long, it looks
> like the superstar wide receiver
> has gotten himself open."

> (CUT TO:)

38. INT. FIELD|EDWARD JONES DOME - NIGHT

-UP ANGLE On the time clock ticking away
in slow motion.

-SEQUENCE OF SHOTS, MICHEAL walking to

his seating section 333 MICHEAL noticing

the two agents are walking towards his

direction along section 325. MICHEAL sits

down quickly behind the fans in front of

him standing up.

(CUT TO:)

**39. INT. TV CAST BOOTH|EDWARD JONES DOME
- NIGHT**

Terry-TV ANNOUNCER 1
(Replying, excited)
"The quarterback breaks left,
Uh oh, here comes the "Big animal"
Oh, he almost sacked by the Cowboys
Line Mr. Defensive player of the year.
He gets it off, He gets it off.."

DOCUMENTED FILE# 000073

(CUT TO:)

40. INT. SIDELINE|EDWARD JONES DOME - NIGHT

-CRANE SHOT, on the football sailing through the air the Rams Wide Receiver and the cornerback are going at it. SLOW MOTION, on The Rams Wide Receiver sprinting straight then starts to slant to the right towards the corner of the End zone LOW WIDE ANGLE, from the opposite angle.

Chris-TV ANNOUNCER 2

(Announcing Cont'd)

"The ball is sailing,

He's going, he going.."

-PANAGLIDE, of the fans in the stands taking a deep breath, hoping their star wide receiver can catch this amazing pass.

(CUT TO:)

41. INT. TV CAST BOOTH|EDWARD JONES DOME - NIGHT

Terry-TV ANNOUNCER 1

(Shouting)

"He leaps in the air"

-FULL SHOT, on the Cowboys cornerback hands barely missing the football by mere inches. The Rams receiver catches the football with his fingers tips rolling the football to his palm for a safe catch.

DOCUMENTED FILE# 000075

-LOW WIDE ANGLE/TIGHT ON, the Rams receiver cleats, watching both of his feet on their toes dragging in the End zone. Just inches away from going out of bounds"

42. INT. SIDELINE|EDWARD JONES DOME - NIGHT

Chris-TV ANNOUNCER 2

(Announcing Cont'd)

"Oh my god, He caught it, ladies and gentleman.

He got it, he got it.

The Rams have tied the game

against the Dallas Cowboys

36-36 with no time left on

the clock in the 4th quarter.

All they have to do is make the

field goal to win the game.

What an amazing game tonight,

the home crowd is going wild."

(CUT TO:)

43. INT. STANDS|EDWARD JONES DOME - NIGHT

-DOLLYING AHEAD, The 2 agents are looking

for MICHEAL Logan. One of the agents puts

his finger near his ear, looking down at

his tracking device. Both agents look up

directly towards MICHEAL, then begin to

toss people out the way to get to MICHEAL.

(CUT TO:)

DOCUMENTED FILE# 000077

-LOW PANAGLIDE, on the Rams kicker as kicks the football towards the field goal to win the game. SEQUENCE OF SHOTS, The agents have closed in on MICHEAL. One of the agents shoots MICHEAL in his wrist but MICHEAL manages to tussle away the gun using martial art moves he didn't even know he had and breaks for the exit near Entry A. At the same time, his memory starts to come back and remembers that these particular assassins are working for the Portal X Facility.

Both agents start shooting THEIR auto-handgun with the MPZ-Silencer inside the arena. Everyone is screaming while the football is going through the field goal. The MPZ-Silencer does not make a sound

when it's shot like the normal silencer.

All we see is what the bullets are coming

in contact with. The agents are shooting

down innocent people in the dome, trying

to kill MICHEAL. People are being hit left

in right as MICHEAL runs for the exit.

(Entry A)

(CUT TO:)

44. INT. STANDS|EDWARD JONES DOME - NIGHT

MICHEAL

(In pain whispering)

"These agents work for Portal X,

damn I'm hit."

DOCUMENTED FILE# 000079

-TIGHT ON, MICHEAL looking down at his wrist bleeding.

MICHEAL

(In pain whispering)

"I got to find out why are they these guys are going to kill me"

(CUT TO:)

45. INT. STAIRWELL|EDWARD JONES DOME - NIGHT

-TIGHT ON, MICHEAL's wrist still bleeding pretty fast, MICHEAL is breathing heavily as he running out of the stadium.

MICHEAL

(In pain)

DOCUMENTED FILE# 000080

"Arrrghhh"

(CUT TO:)

46. INT. ENTRY A|EDWARD JONES DOME – NIGHT

-CRANE SHOT, on MICHEAL stumbling at the exit doors of Entry A. He tucks away his pistol trying blends with some of the crowd that are already leaving. He heads for the parking lot hiding behind a parked car. MICHEAL still breathing heavily to the point to where he is going to pass out. Then out of nowhere CUT FAST, on a gun pointed to the back of his head. It is the same female cop that he ran into from the landing earlier that night! JUMP CUT on Both agents notice MICHEAL

near The police and start walking away in the opposite direction LOW WIDE ANGLE on Jennifer aiming her gun at MICHEAL.

JENNIFER/Female Police Officer

(Shouting)

"Freeze…"

DISSOLVE TO BLACKOUT

47. INT. POLICE SQUAD CAR - NIGHT

-HIGH WIDE SHOT, on the side of the police car. TIGHT ON DASHBOARD, [11pm] on the screen. MICHEAL starts to wake-up in handcuffs behind the cage. While the

DOCUMENTED FILE# 000082

Female police officer is taking him to the station. MICHEAL completely wakes up notices his wrist is bandaged and begins pleading to the cop to let him go...

MICHEAL

(Dazed and confused)

"Where, where, are you taking me?"

JENNIFER/Female Police Officer

(Firm replying)

"I'm taking you

in for questioning,

I am booking you for

assault on a police

officer, and for carrying

a concealed weapon.

By the way,

DOCUMENTED FILE# 000083

my head is still

pounding from hitting

my head of my car.

I was on my way home when

all units received the call.

I saw that you where bleeding so

I got the paramedics to

wrapped your wrist with some bandages.

I was the only patrol unit

in the area with a cage

in my car to escort to the station."

I tried to find your identification,

But I only found a metal rod looking

object you were carrying?

I thought that it was a pen

What is it?

[Transmission-feed break]

DOCUMENTED FILE# 000084

MICHEAL

(Nonchalant)

"It's a long story

Do you usually talk to all

The people you arrest in

The backseat of your car?"

JENNIFER/Female Police Officer

(Replying)

"I work 2 shifts straight,

I got plenty of time and

by the way you are going to

need a hell of a good lawyer

to get you of this mess."

MICHEAL

(Nonchalant)

"I don't need one"

DOCUMENTED FILE# 000085

JENNIFER/Female Police Officer

(Laughing)

"Ha!"

-HIGH WIDE SHOT, on Jennifer pulling into the parking lot of the downtown police precinct.

The ANGLE is a "back shot of the car, with the camera outside the window. MICHEAL starts moving around looking at the police sign. UP ANGLE, The "E" in police flickers on and off as Jennifer is parking the car. She asks MICHEAL another Question.

JENNIFER/Female Police Officer

(Pondering)

"So what are you a big lawyer

DOCUMENTED FILE# 000086

or something?"

MICHEAL

(Replying)

"Nah, I work for the government,

I'm a scientist and engineer"

JENNIFER/Female Police Officer

(Sarcasm)

"Is that so Mr. Big Shot?

well what where you doing with

A gun shooting up a football game.

MICHEAL

(Being honest)

"I took it off one of the people

Who was trying to kill me?"

DOCUMENTED FILE# 000087

-CLOSE ANGLE, on MICHEAL talking to Jennifer, while another police officer knocks on the patrol car window and catches them off guard. TIGHT ON Jennifer winding down the window starting a short conversation while getting her stuff before they head into the police station.

(CUT TO:)

48. EXT. PARKING LOT|POLICE STATION - NIGHT

LISA/Female Police Officer|Dispatcher

"Hey Jenn, is this him?"

-TIGHT ON LISA's HAND, pointing to the back window.

DOCUMENTED FILE# 000088

LISA/Female Police Officer|Dispatcher

(Acting silly)

"Is this the guy

that was shooting up

The Edward Jones Dome?

He doesn't look like

the killer type but I guess

these days you never know.

Anyway I have to run

See ya"

-LOW WIDE ANGLE, on Lisa starting to walk off. She turns around looking through the back window saying her few last to Jennifer before she takes off. At the same time Jennifer is opening the back door to the patrol car.

DOCUMENTED FILE# 000089

LISA/Female Police Officer|Dispatcher

"Let me know what happens

with his one..Adios

JENNIFER/Female Police Officer

"Okay, see you in the morning"

[Transmission-feed break]

LOW WIDE ANGLE, on Jennifer pulling MICHEAL

out the back seat, bringing him into the

police station.

(CUT TO:)

49. INT. QUESTIONING ROOM 2a|POLICE

STATION - EARLY MORNING

-PANNING UP , to a bright light glaring at MICHEAL, The 2 ways mirror shows MICHEAL reflection sitting on a metal chair next to a long table. TIGHT ON, A hot cup of coffee is sitting the left corner of the table, the room is smoked out with a cigarette burning in the ashtray that a cop left while talking to his supervisors outside the door consulting with other officers about why they can find his file in their protocol.

(CUT TO:)

50. INT. POLICE STATION - EARLY MORNING

Captain HARRIS

(Wondering)

DOCUMENTED FILE# 000091

"Who's this guy? Why don't we
Have his prints in our system?,
Jennifer we haven't found
any shell casings in the dome.
All we have are tons of bodies
and no witnesses. We need some
hard evidence on him now"

JENNIFER/Female Police Officer

"Yes Sir"

-ANGLE-MACRO SHOT, on Captain Harris
yelling at other officers in the police
station. Then another officer tell the
captain there where 2 other suspects in
the shooting.

[Transmission-feed break]

DOCUMENTED FILE# 000092

Captain HARRIS

(Irritated)

"Somebody needs to find out what
The hell is going on here. Find those
two other suspects from the Dome stack"

(CUT TO:)

51. INT. QUESTIONING ROOM 2b|POLICE STATION – EARLY MORNING

-TIGHT ON, Jennifer handing Captain Harris the personal items of MICHEAL Logan. Harris opens up his medicine vile and pops a few capsules. They walk into room 2b of the questioning room. They are behind the two-way mirror watching MICHEAL sitting with his head down.

DOCUMENTED FILE# 000093

Captain HARRIS

(Irritated)

"It looks like the only person

who might know some answers

around here is this guy."

JENNIFER/Female Police Officer

(Replying)

"These are his personal belongings

that we found on him Captain."

Captain HARRIS

(Curious)

"This looks like a Auto,

with MPZ-Silencer.

I have never seen one before.

Only Top Level Facility

Agents carry these type

of weapons."

-TIGHT ON, Capt. Harris accidentally pressing a hidden button on the side of the auto-handgun. Harris completely shatters the see through glass with the blast. MICHEAL is knocked back falling to the floor with the amount of force the MPZ-Silencer. Half of the wall in the room is gone revealing the stations parking lot where MICHEAL is located. The Captain and Jennifer cannot believe what just happened. They are dazed from the blast.

Captain HARRIS

(Curious)

"What the hell?

Get him before he bails?

DOCUMENTED FILE# 000095

Somebody Get in there.."

(CUT TO:)

52. INT. QUESTIONING ROOM 2b|POLICE STATION - EARLY MORNING

FULL SHOT on Captain Harris trying to order officers to stop MICHEAL from escaping. At the same time. Two different government Agents appear in the FRAME. Both of them are standing in the middle of the doorway. TIGHT ON both agents showing their identification to Captain Harris.

Captain HARRIS

(Shouting)

"What the hell do you want?"

DOCUMENTED FILE# 000096

TWO UNDERCOVER AGENTS

(Dark, screwed sounding)

"That's classified, we are here to collect Mr. Logan and bring back with us"

(both agents talk in unison)

Captain HARRIS

(Shouting)

"Back with you, Ha! Under whose authority?"

TWO UNDERCOVER AGENTS

(dark, screwed sounding)

"The Portal X Facility"

Captain HARRIS

(Shouting, pissed)

DOCUMENTED FILE# 000097

"The Portal X Facility,

Why wasn't I notified

about this from the

shooting at the stadium

earlier?"

-TIGHT ON, one of the agents throwing the proper detaining paperwork for MICHEAL's retrieval in the face of the Captain. Jennifer looks on wondering what are 2 Portal X Facility doing there for a domestic case.

HANDHELD CAMERA on One agent walking into the questioning room looking directly at MICHEAL and begins to talk.

[Transmission-feed break]

DOCUMENTED FILE# 000098

(CUT TO:)

53. INT. QUESTIONING ROOM 2a|POLICE STATION – EARLY MORNING

UNDERCOVER AGENTS #2

(Dark, screwed, deceiving sounding)

"We apologize for the inconvenience Mr. Logan, its time you come with us"

MICHEAL

"Yeah I bet, so you can kill me"

(CUT TO:)

54. INT. QUESTIONING ROOM 2b|POLICE STATION – EARLY MORNING

DOCUMENTED FILE# 000099

Captain HARRIS

(whispering)

"Mr. Logan, that's his name

Why do they want him dead?"

*TIGHT ON: Captain Harris listening to the conversation...as he notices MICHEAL moving towards the whole in the wall to escape..

(CUT TO:)

55. INT. QUESTIONING ROOM 2a|POLICE STATION - EARLY MORNING

-FULL SHOT, on MICHEAL running towards the hole in the wall, noticing a writing pen lying near the damaged wall. MICHEAL

slides on the floor, grabs a the pen so he can get out of his handcuffs. Then he jumps through the wall into the police parking lot.. The Agents try to shoot MICHEAL down missing again shooting the wall and part of the ceiling down enclosing the them in the room. Both agents look at each other while on the floor and say:

UNDERCOVER AGENTS #1

(dark, screwed, deceiving sounding)

"Where in trouble now"

-CUT FAST, on Both agents running out towards the exit of the police station. One of the agents came back and grabbed the auto-hand gun that Harris was carrying and says:

DOCUMENTED FILE# 0000101

UNDERCOVER AGENTS #2

(Dark, screwed sounding)

"We'll need this for documentation"

(CUT TO:)

**56. EXT. PARKING LOT|POLICE STATION -
EARLY MORNING**

-RESUME WIDE, on both agents hopping in their Crown Victoria after MICHEAL.

(CUT TO:)

**57. INT. QUESTIONING ROOM 2|POLICE STATION
- EARLY MORNING**

FULL SHOT on Jennifer picking up the metal

hypersonic pen that MICHEAL was carrying and goes after MICHEAL as well. Captain Harris looks at one of other officers and the rest of the wall down. After the dust settles, one of the officers, dust the dirt off Captain's Hat and it fall apart. The Capt. looks at the supervisor and says:

Captain HARRIS

(Shouting)

"Why I aww ta,

what the...

hell are you doing?"

-TIGHT ON, Captain Harris starts talking to the officers in the room with him…

[Transmission-feed break]

DOCUMENTED FILE# 0000103

Captain HARRIS

(Pondering)

"I need you guys

to figure out why do those

Portal X Agents want

this Logan so bad.

These guys showed up pretty fast,

a little too fast if you

know what I mean.

Something smells fishy

about this whole situation

that went down.

I want you to figure out

what the hell is going on

I'm too old for this shit."

(CUT TO:)

DOCUMENTED FILE# 0000104

58. EXT. STREETS OF ST. LOUIS - MORNING

-RESUME WIDE, on the agents heading towards the Circle District of America.. (Rest of the USA outside of Missouri). Both agents believe that this will be the only location MICHEAL would be heading to hide.

(CUT TO:)

59. INT. STREETS OF ST. LOUIS - MORNING

-TIGHT ON Jennifer driving around St. Louis City, not knowing that MICHEAL has been hiding underneath a black blanket in the back seat of her patrol car ever since he escaped from the police station. At the same time, LISA came back to work

DOCUMENTED FILE# 0000105

the early morning shift as dispatcher,
and begins he duty.

LISA/Female Police Officer|Dispatcher

[Audio Voice]
"This is Dispatcher 579 dash 37.
Calling all cars, head to the
entrance of the Circle District.
Be on the look out for a suspect:
Male, 5'9, Possibly armed
and dangerous with a blue
shirt, blue jeans."

-TIGHT ON, Jennifer pressing the respond
button on her receiver to talk back to
Lisa.

*FX "BEEP"

DOCUMENTED FILE# 0000106

JENNIFER/Female Police Officer

"I read you loud in clear

Dispatcher 579 Dash 37,

I am going into the Circle District"

Lisa responding back to Jennifer directly...

LISA/Female Police Officer|Dispatcher

[Audio Voice]

"You are going to do what?

You are going to get yourself

killed out there.

Traveling out of our boundary

lines is not good for any cop.

Inside the Circle District

they go by their own rules.

Be cautious of the gangs out there,

DOCUMENTED FILE# 0000107

Oh wait a minute, look at your

Console screen, right now.

-TIGHT ON, Jennifer's Main console screen

on her dashboard. It is Lisa on screen

about to patch the captain in for a special

report to all officers looking for MICHEAL.

LISA/Female Police Officer|Dispatcher

(O.S.)

(Reporting)

"This is Dispatcher 579 dash 37.

Capt. Harris has received

some confidential files about

the fugitive on the loose."

JUMP CUT, of Captain Harris patches

on the screen.. MICHEAL happens to be

DOCUMENTED FILE# 0000108

listening in on the conversation eager
to find out more about his past..

Captain HARRIS (O.S.)

(Reporting)

"Everyone listen up, I have found
out that ever since 2010.
MICHEAL W. Logan, scientist engineer,
even an ex-soldier has discovered
that he could physically transport
humans, large objects through the
Gateway Arch using Sound, light
and motion. He even designed the
Energy Peras (cars) we drive today,
everything is classified in the
Portal X Facility, It is a fortress.
All we could find out is that
the Portal X Facility wants no

DOCUMENTED FILE# 0000109

one to know about it

not even the police administration.

Do not speak or tell anyone about

what I have told you. Be safe

Out there and good luck."

(CUT TO:)

60. EXT. ENTRANCE - THE CIRCLE DISTRICT OF AMERICA - DAY

-HIGH WIDE SHOT, on Jennifer a few blocks away from The Circle District. She notices that the motorcycle gang named the Assassinationz are parked near the entrance to the Circle District from the other side. Jennifer looks right at the rusted entrance sign labeled "Welcome to

DOCUMENTED FILE# 0000110

The Circle District"

(CUT TO:)

61. THE CIRCLE DISTRICT OF AMERICA - DAY

-RESUME WIDE, Jennifer continues forward and the Assassinationz just let her drive by into The Circle District. Since there are 6 dead mini guns that will shooting down anything not authorized to enter St. Louis City.

LISA/Female Police Officer|Dispatcher

[Audio Voice]

(Worried)

"Jenn, we have all the cars

low jacked, so I can pin point

DOCUMENTED FILE# 0000111

your position at anytime.

Remember, do not mess with

Streets' Property,

he Run The Circle District

like his baby. I heard the Gov't is

trying to handle the problem but

the people that do still live out there

are in his control.

The on-screen database

will not work once you pass

a mile thru in the Circle

District. So contact me via

radio if you need me.

And remember, Xavier Street

sometimes refers to himself as

the Street President. Why?

Because he know everything coming in

and out of his District. So keep a low

profile in the Circle District. Which
makes up all of the United States except
for St. Louis City.
After the recession came the depression.
& After the depression came of energy
wars.. Xavier was a businessman who
bought all of the outside boundaries in
2020. He has total control of energy
power in The Circle District. He
practically bought the entire United
States as we know it.
The government started running out
of money as you already know.
They were looking for buyers for the
American soil and Xavier stepped in and
bought it all. Our President even gave
him the original white house.
I heard he later pulled it up and

DOCUMENTED FILE# 0000113

transported it to a secret location.
It has been said that he put
the White House under an abandoned
mansion Somewhere in the Circle District.
Can you believe he put it underground?

JENNIFER/Female Police Officer

(Replying back)

"Yeah I heard that's crazy.
I will radio back when I can"

(CUT TO:)

**62. EXT. DEAD ROAD - THE CIRCLE DISTRICT
OF AMERICA - DAY**

-HIGH WIDE SHOT, on Jennifer driving down
Dead Road in the Circle District. She

passes up dead animals along the side and in the middle of the road. Jennifer starts pulling out the hypersonic pen that MICHEAL was carrying looking at it in her hand. She pushed a button for the cage to go down. Then she hears something moving in her back seat..

JENNIFER/Female Police Officer

(Curious)

What the?"

(CUT TO:)

63. INT. POLICE SQUAD CAR - THE CIRCLE DISTRICT OF AMERICA - DAY

DOCUMENTED FILE# 0000115

-TIGHT ON, MICHEAL getting up quickly grabbing the hypersonic pen out of Jennifer's hand. With his other hand grabbing her gun on the front seat pointing it towards her neck.

JENNIFER/Female Police Officer

(Curious)

"What the hell?"

MICHEAL

(Alarming)

"Don't move and don't radio in.
I am not going to hurt you,
just drive to Xavier Streets
House now!"

[Transmission-feed break]

JENNIFER/Female Police Officer

(Slightly frightened)

"No, I can't, they won't let me back to St. Louis City if I help you. Plus, I don't even know where it's located okay!"

(Jenn acting emotional)

MICHEAL

"I do, it's off the Devil's Highway," -TIGHT ON, MICHEAL shoving the gun into Jennifer's neck after she stares at Micheal. She wants to refuse, but then agrees.

JENNIFER/Female Police Officer

(Slightly frightened)

"Okay, okay, alright, I will take you, I guess you are the killer type. I never heard of the Devil's Highway"

DOCUMENTED FILE# 0000117

[Transmission-feed break]

(CUT TO:)

64. EXT. DEVIL'S HIGHWAY - THE CIRCLE DISTRICT OF AMERICA - MIDDAY

-FULL SHOT, on the Patrol car going through The Circle District. MICHEAL does not answer right away, so Jennifer starts driving in the direction MICHEAL points her to go. After a while, MICHEAL starts a conversation to waste time until they reach Xavier's Estate.

MICHEAL

"I'm going to let the world know the truth about the Portal X

DOCUMENTED FILE# 0000118

Facility. I remembering now only in
flashbacks. The world we live
in has been manipulated,
by programming our minds
so they have total control..
"Why do you think they sold the
Nations Energy to Xavier Streets.
That's because the Portal X Facility
uses around 89% of the nation's energy.
The other 11% is controlled by Xavier,
that's why he decided to have a power
limit for each home in
The Circle District except
for his estate. The Real reason
why they want me dead,
I know the truth about a new
world, just like earth.

DOCUMENTED FILE# 0000119

JENNIFER/Female Police Officer

(Questioning)

"A new world, what do you mean?"

-COVERGING DOLLY, on Jennifer pulling aside on the outer rim of Xavier Streets Estate, MICHEAL looks at Jennifer and starts talking.

(CUT TO:)

65. INT. POLICE SQUAD CAR - THE CIRCLE DISTRICT OF AMERICA - MIDDAY

MICHEAL

"The Gateway Arch, it's a portal to get to Planet X, a planet just

like ours with animals water oxygen the works. Only is it doesn't have any humans living on it."

(CUT TO:)

66. EXT. XAVIER STREET'S ESTATE - MIDDAY

-CUT FAST on MICHEAL getting out of the car, point to Jennifer to pop the trunk. TIGHT ON, Jennifer reaching on the steering wheel, pressing the trunk button.
-ANGLE REVERSE, on MICHEAL walking to the trunk of the patrol car bending down picking up some arsenal gear, and weapons. -LOW PANAGLIDE, on the side of the car. Jennifer steps out walking towards MICHEAL.

DOCUMENTED FILE# 0000121

JENNIFER/Female Police Officer

(Persuading)

"Take me with you"

MICHEAL

"I can't, I'm sorry, go home.

This is my problem now"

JENNIFER/Female Police Officer

(Shouting)

"What do you think Xavier is

going to do for you?

Help you?

That will be the last thing

he will do, even I know that.

Once he bought the Circle District

he doesn't trust anyone but himself.

DOCUMENTED FILE# 0000122

Plus it's a fortress, you won't make it

in there without some help."

Micheal

"He's the only one with enough

resources to help me. If you

want to come, you can come.

Just let me do all of the talking.

Ditch the car behind those hills

over there. Change you clothes as

well. That police uniform will

get both of us killed.

(Being sarcastic)

*MICHEAL telling Jennifer on the attack

plan to get into The Xavier Estate

JENNIFER/Female Police Officer

"Okay, I want to find out what

the hell is going on around here

anyway. It's about time my life

had a little action.."

                              (CUT TO:)

67. EXT. FRONTGATE|XAVIER STREET'S ESTATE

- MIDDAY

-AERIAL SHOT ON, Jennifer walking up to

Xavier Streets Estate. Jennifer notices an

army Jeep approaching the gate.

-CRANE SHOT of the army jeep stopping at

the gate.

-PANNING UP ON, Jennifer legs, hips and

rubbing her chest. TIGHT ON, The guard

starting to swirl the tooth pick in his

mouth as he is sizing up Jennifer's body.

DOCUMENTED FILE# 0000124

-WHIP PANNING ON, Jennifer flirting with the guard, distracting him while MICHEAL sneaks in the Estate.

JENNIFER/Female Police Officer

(Flirting)

"Hey big boy, I'm a little lost but I guess there is always time to have a little fun.."

XAVIER's SECURITY GUARD #1

(Smirking)

"Hey pretty lady, it has been a long time since I had some action around here.."

-LOW PANAGLIDE, on MICHEAL sneaking down

the side of the estate. MICHEAL reaches the gate, looking around for the security cameras. -CUT FAST ON, MICHEAL breaking out a spray can of liquid Nitrogen, then starts spraying the fence with it.

-CUT FAST, on Jennifer swinging her hair while bending over rubbing her hips back and forth keeping the security guards busy at the front gate.

-WHIP PANNING, on MICHEAL breaking through the gate, sneaking towards the front gate behind the guard, then slams both guards Heads on the side of the army jeep. Jennifer looks at MICHEAL and begins to speak.

JENNIFER/Female Police Officer

(Sarcastic)

"Looks like you smash people's

heads on cars for a living?"

MICHEAL

(Sarcastic)

"Didn't I tell you

I like to play rough.

Come on, let go"

BLACKOUT

68. EXT. XAVIER STREET'S ESTATE – MIDDAY

MICHEAL

(Pondering)

"Where is everybody?"

JENNIFER/Female Police Officer

(replying)

DOCUMENTED FILE# 0000127

"I don't know, this is weird".

MICHEAL

"Xavier has to be here,

I heard he never leaves because

he's scared of getting assassinated."

-HANDHELD CAMERA, on MICHEAL and Jennifer reaching the side of the mansion. They both duck down in front of a Mercedes-Benz noticing one of the security cameras panning there way on the top of the house..

MICHEAL

"Get down!"

-UP ANGLE ON, the security camera passing

DOCUMENTED FILE# 0000128

by again, MICHEAL wipes the sweat from his face and says..

MICHEAL

(Whispering)

"There must be a way in

here without being seen.."

JENNIFER/Female Police Officer

(replying)

"I got a idea.."

MICHEAL

(Whispering)

"What!, what the hell

are you going to do?"

[Transmission-feed break]

-HIGH WIDE ANGLE, on the security camera turning away from their location. TIGHT ON, Jennifer trying to open the door to Mercedes-Benz and notices that the door is unlocked, Jennifer glances at MICHEAL raising her eyebrows. They both quickly hop in the car avoiding the security camera panning back their way…

(CUT TO:)

69. INT. MERCEDES-BENZ|XAVIER STREET'S ESTATE - MIDDAY

MICHEAL

"What are you doing now?"

[Transmission-feed break]

DOCUMENTED FILE# 0000130

JENNIFER/Female Police Officer

"I wasn't always a cop, I used to hot-wire cars with my guys friends when I was a teenager just for fun driving around town. I was young tom boy. Good thing I never got caught."

-TIGHT ON, Jennifer pulling out the wires from under the dash. Jennifer places a small computer on the dashboard to stop the Mercedes on-board computer from locking up and sounding the alarm. She presses the automatic start button near the steering wheel and the car starts up. LOW WIDE ANGLE, on Jennifer driving down 50 feet from the mansion and does a complete 360 and starts driving the car directly towards the front door of Xavier's Mansion.

DOCUMENTED FILE# 0000131

MICHEAL

(Screaming)

"Are you nuts?
You're going to get us
both killed."

JENNIFER/Female Police Officer

(Smiling)

"You might want to Buckle up"

RESUME WIDE ON, Jennifer aiming for the door ramp and drives directly though the front door, smashing anything it comes in contact with inside of the house, then lands directly inside the water fountain inside of the house.

JENNIFER/Female Police Officer

DOCUMENTED FILE# 0000132

"Well, where in, let's go "

-LOW ANGLE ON, MICHEAL and Jennifer getting outside the car. By the time they look up, there are tons of Xaviers Security guards aiming automatic machines guns at them. Jennifer looks at MICHEAL and says:

JENNIFER/Female Police Officer

(Joking)

"Maybe we should have knocked"

ESTATE SECURITY GUARDS #2

(Shouting)

"GET OUT OF THE CAR NOW"

BLACKOUT

DOCUMENTED FILE# 0000133

(CUT TO:)

70. INT. ELEVATOR SHAFT|XAVIER STREET'S ESTATE - MIDDAY

ANGLE BETWEEN TWO OF, Xavier's Guards escorting Jennifer and MICHEAL into the elevator. The elevator ceiling has one of the original Presidential seals from the white house. The bottom of the elevator shaft is see through. Jennifer and MICHEAL look at each completely shocked about what they might see below.

          JENNIFER/Female Police Officer

               (Thinking in her head)
          "Is the original white house here?
          I was wonder what Xavier and his gang

are doing with all these powerful
resources?"

-TIGHT ON, MICHEAL thinking to himself as
well, he looks over to Jennifer while she
is looking down the elevator shaft.

MICHEAL

(Thinking)
"I wish I never told her
to come with me.
I got her involved in this mess
I got to think of a
plan real fast!"

-CLOSE UP, on MICHEAL looking at Jennifer
with a little more feeling.

DOCUMENTED FILE# 0000135

MICHEAL

(Thinking in his head)

"I never really noticed how

beautiful she is."

CUT FAST ON, the digital elevator display.
The display begins to speak as they are
approaching their destination underneath
ground.

ELEVATOR [Audio Voice]

(Automated)

"Approaching 2100 hundred

feet below sea level, in 5 seconds..

5.4.3.2.1. Destination reached"

(CUT TO:)

71. INT. THE WHITE HOUSE|UNDERGROUND - NIGHT

-TIGHT ON, the elevator coming to a halt. The doors slide open using compressed air technology. Both security guards push MICHEAL & Jennifer into the Green Room. There are frames of money from all around the world on the left side of the wall. On the right side of the wall are almost all the pictures of the ten most dangerous places on Earth: Russia, Brazil, South Africa, Burundi, Antarctica, Afghanistan, Somalia, Sudan, Columbia and Iraq. The guards push Jennifer and MICHEAL to enter the doors straight ahead. All the guards fall back and MICHEAL opens up the doors to see the original white house office of the President. There is a tall chair with a character sitting it in, facing the opposite direction. The chairs starts to turn around with Xavier Street sitting down smiling at them and begins to speak.

Xavier Street's|THE PRESIDENT

TO THE CIRCLE DISTRICT OF AMERICA

"Greetings, Welcome to the White House, do you like what I have done with the place? I knew the government was out of their minds trying to sell the entire land of our nation. So when the opportunity came along I had to seize it, but... I'm sure you are here for more important reasons than to hear me talk about being a tyrant figure. But since you where driving one of my

favorite cars through the front of my mansion above,oh yes, there must be a good explanation why you are here. Plus I knew you where coming the whole time, the Assassinationz tipped me off that they where looking for MICHEAL in The Circle District.. "

-PANAGLIDE ON, Jennifer squinting her eyes at Xavier while MICHEAL takes a few steps forward to ask Xavier a few questions.

MICHEAL

(Politely)

"I need your help"

Xavier Street's|THE PRESIDENT

TO THE CIRCLE DISTRICT OF AMERICA

(Sarcastically)

DOCUMENTED FILE# 0000139

"You need my help?,

Well I need your help as well"

-TIGHT ON, Xavier pressing a red button underneath his desk, the red curtain behind him starts to slide apart.
MICHEAL and Jennifer look ahead and see something that shocks them completely..

                              (CUT TO:)

72. INT. UNDERGROUND CHAMBER|THE WHITE HOUSE - NIGHT

-LOW WIDE ANGLE, on MICHEAL noticing a map sitting on Xavier's desk, of the Earth and the unfinished measurement codes leading to Planet X sitting on Xavier's Desk.

MICHEAL looks up and slowly gets out of his seat while he notices a 3rd gateway arch in the chamber ahead.

Xavier Street's|THE PRESIDENT
TO THE CIRCLE DISTRICT OF AMERICA

"It must be my lucky day today, I was able to get all the information I needed from various sources within the Portal X Facility to completely build a Portal of mine own. The only thing I was not sure of was how I was going to get someone to activate it by finishing the code for me. You see this particular portal does not need the hypersonic pen you require on the other two. I have constructed a Digital pad that activates

and deactivates this particular portal."

-HIGH PANAGLIDE ON, Xavier's guards pushing MICHEAL and Jennifer into the lower section of the underground chamber. MICHEAL notices that the 3rd gateway is 74% smaller than the one on Planet X and St. Louis, Missouri.

Xavier Street's|THE PRESIDENT

TO THE CIRCLE DISTRICT OF AMERICA

(Curious)

"So what do you think of the 3rd Gateway?"

MICHEAL

(Sarcastic)

"It's a mini me"

DOCUMENTED FILE# 0000142

Xavier Street's|THE PRESIDENT
TO THE CIRCLE DISTRICT OF AMERICA

"I see you still have a sense of humor,
Mr. Logan, I need you to open the portal
for me"

Briefly pausing..

Xavier Street's|THE PRESIDENT
TO THE CIRCLE DISTRICT OF AMERICA

"Anyway if you do so.
I will let you and your
pretty young thing go free,
a favor for a favor!
That's what I will do for you"

JENNIFER/Female Police Officer

"MICHEAL don't trust him, it's a set up."

-PAN ON, Xavier looking at Jennifer with disgust. He hates to be cut off when he speaks. So Xavier starts to discipline Jennifer to get MICHEAL to activate the portal.

Xavier Street's|THE PRESIDENT

TO THE CIRCLE DISTRICT OF AMERICA

(Screaming very loudly

talking to his guards)

"Silence her, and bring her to me."

-PANAGLIDE ON, Xavier's guards grabbing Jennifer, bringing her to a metal table near the side of the chamber. Another huge guard grabs MICHEAL, holding him so he cannot interfere. One of Xavier's guards

DOCUMENTED FILE# 0000144

brings a old vintage wooden box and hands
it to Xavier.

Xavier Street's|THE PRESIDENT

TO THE CIRCLE DISTRICT OF AMERICA

(Shouting)

"Don't speak, when I'm speaking,
I do not allow anyone to over talk
me while in my presence.."

-PAN ON, Xavier is pulling out a futuristic
glove out of a vintage wooden box. Jennifer
and MICHEAL look on.

Xavier Street's|THE PRESIDENT

TO THE CIRCLE DISTRICT OF AMERICA

"Do you know what is in this box.
Well this box was originally owned by

DOCUMENTED FILE# 0000145

The Joseon Dynasty in Korean during the 1700's. It was showcased in the San Francisco Museum. I thought it would be a nice treasure to have ever since I bought the Rest Of America. Anyway, I chose to keep something special inside of it, that you will like very much."

-TIGHT ON, Xavier opening the box pulling out a pair of black gloves with lights on the palms that he starts to slide on..

JENNIFER/Female Police Officer

(Joking)

"Let me guess, it's your stove top glove for baking cookies.."

[Transmission-feed break]

Xavier Street's|THE PRESIDENT

DOCUMENTED FILE# 0000146

TO THE CIRCLE DISTRICT OF AMERICA

"Hahaha, No, these gloves uses an

electrical current that disrupts

the voluntary control

of your muscles.

Something like a

taser but a little more nasty.

I can upgrade up to

four 4 different settings

for discipline between

50 and 2000kv. I will ask

you one more time to

give me the activation codes

or watch me shock your

pretty friend to death."

CAMERA TRACKS, on Xavier shocking Jennifer

with the lowest setting #3. MICHEAL is

DOCUMENTED FILE# 0000147

screaming for Xavier to stop.

JENNIFER/Female Police Officer

"Arrrgghhhhh...Noooooòooo,

stop, please stop!!!!"

-COVERGING DOLLY, on MICHEAL looking at
Jennifer being shocked was too much to
bear. MICHEAL gives in the Xavier's plans.

MICHEAL

(screaming)

"Stop it, your killing her,

Okay, okay,

I will do whatever you want.

Just leave her alone,

Please!!!"

Xavier Street's|THE PRESIDENT

TO THE CIRCLE DISTRICT OF AMERICA

"Please is the magic word,

Mr. Logan. I am not a animal,

just a tyrant, come this way…"

BLACKOUT

73. INT. OBSERVATION ROOM|UNDERGROUND CHAMBER - NIGHT

-HANDHELD CAMERA, FOLLOW Xavier and MICHEAL to the Observation room on the side of the Portal. Two of Xavier's guards carry Jennifer knocked out behind them. TIGHT ON, Xavier explaining his future plans for the 3rd Portal.

MICHEAL

DOCUMENTED FILE# 0000149

"So what are you trying to do?

How did you build a

3rd Gateway Arch here?"

Xavier Street's|THE PRESIDENT

TO THE CIRCLE DISTRICT OF AMERICA

"Remember my obedience code, Mr. Logan. I don't allow anyone to speak until they are spoken to, or given permission. This will be a warning this time, since I cannot have you knock out like your friend back there, you will be useless…"

-TIGHT ON, MICHEAL giving Xavier a dirty look. He walks into a glass room on the side of the portal and Xavier points to where MICHEAL must enter the sequencing codes. MICHEAL walks over to the console.

He begins pressing in the long sequence on the keypad. The portal begins to open up and Xavier stares on with amazement. CLOSE UP, on MICHEAL starts talking to himself.

Xavier Street's|THE PRESIDENT

TO THE CIRCLE DISTRICT OF AMERICA

(Whispering

to himself)

"Holy mother of God. Yes,

the Gateway is finally opening"

-SEQUENCE OF SHOTS, on a satellite in space turning on.. Tracking the portals energy source and within a few minutes, the security alarm going off, with lights

flashing red on the wall.

The Portal X Facility agents are appearing on the security cameras storming into the mansion above shooting Xavier's guards. They begin making their way to the elevator shaft. Jennifer starts coming around from being knocked out. At the same time Xavier's starts rallying up his men to go through the portal.

JENNIFER/Female Police Officer

(curious,

talking to herself)

"How did these agents get

here so fast, they must be

Something I still know,

that they do not have?"

DOCUMENTED FILE# 0000152

Xavier Street's|THE PRESIDENT

TO THE CIRCLE DISTRICT OF AMERICA

"Let's go we are going through the portal. Let's get out of here"

-SEQUENCE OF SHOTS, on Xavier grabbing his reinforcements telling Jennifer and MICHEAL to hop in the Artillery vehicle's to head towards the portal. Xavier's guards set bombs to go off in 60 seconds.

Xavier Street's|THE PRESIDENT

TO THE CIRCLE DISTRICT OF AMERICA

"Where going to Planet X, gentlemen, where going to takeover the Planet X Facility, let's go"

-TIGHT ON, Xavier looking back at MICHEAL in the vehicle

DOCUMENTED FILE# 0000153

Xavier Street's|THE PRESIDENT
TO THE CIRCLE DISTRICT OF AMERICA

(Smiling)

"By the way, I got a big secret

to tell you, when we get there"

-ANGLE REVERSE ON, the agents making their

way through the white house.

The Xavier set up goes off killing all

of the agents, while they ride through the

portal. AERIAL SHOT of The Estate blowing

up...

(CUT TO:)

FADE IN

74. INT. PLANET X FACILITY

-PANAGLIDE ON, Xavier and his guards, Jennifer, MICHEAL arriving through portal to the Planet X Facility. Everyone notices that there is no one in sight as they arrive. Xavier's guards quickly jump out of the vehicles securing the perimeter. SEQUENCE OF SHOTS metallic sounds, green lights flickering, dark blue lasers near the exits..

JENNIFER/Female Police Officer

"This is your secret?,

an abandoned Facility

on Planet X!"

Xavier Street's|THE PRESIDENT

DOCUMENTED FILE# 0000155

TO THE CIRCLE DISTRICT OF AMERICA

"Well, well, well,

she still talks

when not spoken too.

This time I will not

have to shock you,

I have arranged a

meeting to give

you back to the Gov't.

You both have been fooled.

MICHEAL you should of listened

to Jennifer, Guards get them."

-FULL SHOT ON, Xavier's security guards aiming their automatic machine guns towards them both, while holding them both in place.

MICHEAL

DOCUMENTED FILE# 0000156

"Get off me, you set us up

you bastard, there's no one

here anyway, what are you going

to do to us?"

JUMP CUT ON, Jennifer looking right and noticing a shadow from the distance walking towards them from the distant passageway.

THE PRESIDENT OF THE UNITED STATES

"I wouldn't say that is entirely true?"

-WHIP PANNING ON, MICHEAL looking at the President as if he has seen ghost..

MICHEAL

"Mr. President...how could you?"

THE PRESIDENT OF THE UNITED STATES

DOCUMENTED FILE# 0000157

"No one is going to kill me MICHEAL,

right Xavier? I set you up Mr. Logan.

Matter of fact I am going

to send a bomb back

to Earth, that will

wipe out every single human

being on earth.

A special biological weapon

that will enter the blood stream

killing any human within

fifthteen seconds.

Why do you think we erased your

memory and dumped you in at

gas station, so you couldn't

stop my final plans,

but I guess your

memory did recover"

-PANNING UP ON, the screen on the wall,

DOCUMENTED FILE# 0000158

demonstrating how the ball will affect

Earth.

JENNIFER/Female Police Officer

"Mr. President, how can you, I mean

how can you kill all those innocent

People. What did they ever do to you?"

THE PRESIDENT OF THE UNITED STATES

"Innocent, humans on Earth

aren't innocent.

They are sinful.

Don't forgot, even God

wanted to kill all of

mankind long ago,

that is why Planet X

will be the New X World Order.

I will cleanse

DOCUMENTED FILE# 0000159

mother earth of all

its sins and figure out

what I want to do

with it then.

When the stories are

written for this world

down the generations I will

be known as the real God who

created all life on this planet

from my bloodline.

Oh, by the way before I forget,

it's time for Xavier to get his

prize for bringing me MICHEAL Logan."

Xavier Street's|THE PRESIDENT

TO THE CIRCLE DISTRICT OF AMERICA

"Prize? What freaking prize?

You told me that I would

run earth after you sent the

bomb back to kill everyone."

THE PRESIDENT OF THE UNITED STATES

(Evil sounding)

"Oh yes I did promise you Earth

didn't I, well, I thought that you might

like a place better than Earth to live".

Xavier Street's|THE PRESIDENT

TO THE CIRCLE DISTRICT OF AMERICA

"What the hell are you talking about?"

-WHIP PANNING ON, two agents with sniper

rifles above them take out both of Xavier's

guards and then the President walks up to

Xavier and says:

DOCUMENTED FILE# 0000161

THE PRESIDENT OF THE UNITED STATES

(Evil sounding)

"Like Hell!"

TIGHT ON|SLOW MOTION, on a bullet being shot by one of the agents as it travels through the chamber, out of the barrel, into the air and hitting Xavier right between the eyes. The President looks over Xavier's body and to say a few last words..

THE PRESIDENT OF THE UNITED STATES

"You were reckless and stupid Xavier. I always knew that he wanted to take me down..I only needed him to convince you to open the 3rd portal but I guess we where a little too late since he wanted to blow it up, a man who only cares

DOCUMENTED FILE# 0000162

about money is no man at all."

-LOW WIDE ANGLE ON, The president kicking Xavier's dead body, spitting on him.

[Transmission-feed break]

THE PRESIDENT OF THE UNITED STATES

"I guess your plans to kill
me after all failed, Ha"

-CAMERA TRACKS ON, MICHEAL and Jennifer standing in shock. Both agents come down from the level above and point their guns towards Jennifer and MICHEAL. Then the President begins to walk over and kiss Jennifer on the lips roughly. Jennifer tries to push the President off from

kissing her, but fails.

JENNIFER/Female Police Officer

"Get off me you psycho.."

-CUT FAST ON, Jennifer trying to break loose from the guards once more as the President's heads to send the bomb back to Earth.

MICHEAL

(Screaming)

"Don't touch her, get off of her..."

-LOW WIDE ANGLE, on one of the agents punching MICHEAL in the mouth with the butt of his pistol. The President sets the

portal destination back to the Portal X Facility back in St. Louis City. At the same time, MICHEAL kicks the agent in the chest and rushes towards The President to stop him from destroying the world.

-WHIP PANNING ON, The President turning around at the right time and throwing MICHEAL over his shoulder through the portal back to the Earth..

                    MICHEAL

                  (Screaming)

                  "Nooooo!"

-FULL SHOT ON, MICHEAL falling through the portal landing back into The St. Louis Portal Facility. Before MICHEAL can get back up to jump back though the Portal, The

DOCUMENTED FILE# 0000165

President deactivates the portal leaving MICHEAL stranded on Earth. Jennifer falls to her knees crying her heart out..

THE PRESIDENT OF THE UNITED STATES

"Ahh, get up, Jennifer.
You will love me
within time, I will make
sure of that.
Become my wife and bare
the first child
ever born on Planet X."

JENNIFER/Female Police Officer

"I will never be your wife,
you're out of your mind,
I will never marry you. Never."

-CRANE SHOT ON, Jennifer spitting in the President's face. FOLLOW the agents taking her away to the Mind Control Lab. The President looks through the screen on the wall, showing a picture of the galaxy he is in now. He glares at it for a second and then heads towards to his elevator to his private quarters.

BLACKOUT

75. INT. PORTAL X FACILITY - PORTAL X AREA - LEVEL 2

-RESUME WIDE ON, MICHEAL Inside the Portal X Facility in St. Louis City, The building is completely filled with Agents. He jumps

DOCUMENTED FILE# 0000167

to the right behind a pillar as 2 agents walk right in front of him. MICHEAL grabs both guards from behind, snapping their necks and pulls them behind the pillar into a storage area.

MICHEAL takes the clothes off one of the guard including his identification card, which reads STL-PXF #314-546.

-FOLLOW MICHEAL walking out the storage area pulling his hat down and heading towards the front Entrance.. A Facility Agent spots MICHEAL pulling his cap down and starts walking towards MICHEAL.

PORTAL X FACILITY TOP SECURITY AGENT

"Stop there! State your #?"

CLOSE-UP on MICHEAL with the guard

over his shoulder. MICHEAL is looking skeptical but going along not trying to be noticed..

MICHEAL

"#314-546"

TIGHT ON-SCREEN, The Top Agent checking his log sheet for personnel. The Agent notices that MICHEAL is looking a little impatient and begins to slowly reach for his gun when his on-screen data screen lights up, showing that an unidentified suspect is located within facility and must be found. The top agent looks at MICHEAL, but is distracted by another agent running towards him asking him to do a perimeter search of the building.

DOCUMENTED FILE# 0000169

The Top agent looks at MICHEAL and let him go, while ordering all of the guards to begin searching for suspect.

PORTAL X FACILITY TOP SECURITY AGENT

"Everything check outs
Agent #314-546, You may proceed"

MICHEAL

"Yes sir"

-HANDHELD CAMERA ON, MICHEAL walking threw the front rotating doors. The new futuristic metro link is pulling up, MICHEAL hops on and looks at the map. He notices that his childhood friend Henry Blades House in the Circle District not to far away...The train departs towards the

DOCUMENTED FILE# 0000170

Circle district.

BLACKOUT

76. INT. METROLINK TRAIN - DAY

-ANGLE BETWEEN THE SEATS ON THE TRAIN
SHOWING, MICHEAL riding the Metrolink to
the Circle District. It's powered by free
Energy. (Usually only lower class workers
for the Gov't use the Metro link to clean
the inside of the buildings)..Its the only
train allowed to pass into St. Louis City,
from the Circle District.

BILL/METROLINK TRAIN ANNOUNCER/OPERATOR

[Audio/Radio Voice]

"Next stop...Desert Drive

DOCUMENTED FILE# 0000171

Last Stop, Final Stop!...Thank you"

MICHEAL

(Aggravated)

"I don't have much time"

-LOW WIDE ANGLE, on MICHEAL fixing his shoe strings, he looks right towards the train door window 2 cars down and notices that two Portal X Agents: Number 2.0 and 3.5 are coming his way. Agent 3.5 looks towards other passengers scanning their eyes for identification as they walk through the train.

(*AGENT 2.0 AND 3.5 are Government Funded Neo Machines)

DOCUMENTED FILE# 0000172

PORTAL X FACILITY AGENT NUMBER 2.0

(Female voice)

"Scanning, Subject MICHEAL W. Logan

Termination highest priority"

-ON SCREEN, Agent's 3.5 scanning device, randomly beeping, starting a slow circle pattern. CLOSE-UP on a train passenger starting to talk to MICHEAL about the agents.

Weazel/METROLINK PASSENGER

"Whoa a real life Agent 3.5

a perfect weapon."

A real living human being

with a machine skeleton kinda like

a Terminator huh?

DOCUMENTED FILE# 0000173

MICHEAL

"Who the hell are you?"

Weazel/METROLINK PASSENGER

(Replying)

"My name is Weazel,

cause I can weasel

out of anything"

TIGHT ON|ON SCREEN, the television inside the train displaying the news on the train. MICHEAL's face hits the front screen during the news for being wanted by the police in St. Louis City for killing Xavier Street's. CUT FAST ON, MICHEAL getting up quickly, taking a phone away from a lawyer that was talking to his client. The lawyer gets up outraged and tries to get his

phone back from MICHEAL. MICHEAL turns around and knocks the lawyer completely out. Weazel stands up and looks at the lawyer and says:

Weazel/METROLINK PASSENGER

"You got knocked the hell out, fool"

-WHIP PANNING ON, MICHEAL walking towards the front on the train where the operator is located.

Weazel/METROLINK PASSENGER

(Curious)

"Hey there are looking for

you aren't they?"

DOCUMENTED FILE# 0000175

-CUT FAST, on MICHEAL stopping in front of the operator's door. He looks back and the camera zooms in as both Portal X Facility Agents are entering the train car Micheal has ran into.

MICHEAL opens the operator's door to get inside and take control of the train since the operator forgot to lock it.

77. INT. OPERATORS CABIN|METROLINK TRAIN - DAY

BILL/METROLINK TRAIN ANNOUNCER/OPERATOR

"Hey, get out of here, you punk."

[Transmission-feed break]

DOCUMENTED FILE# 0000176

-TIGHT ON, The announcer pulling out his shotgun from behind his pants. MICHEAL pulls the gun out of the operator's hands so fast that he jumps back leaning again the controls and putting them on the same track as the Speedora train ahead.

BILL/METROLINK TRAIN ANNOUNCER/OPERATOR

"You damn fool, you got us headed towards other train and a Speedora at that! The Government made those train indestructible.
We're headed right for it, Dear god!"

-HIGH WIDE SHOT, on both trains heading towards each other, closer and closer MICHEAL and Bill look on thinking that

DOCUMENTED FILE# 0000177

they are about to die but both trains pass each other by. MICHEAL looks at Bill and says:

MICHEAL

"Either you must be drunk, or too old. Or you where already headed towards the train old man. Maybe, I should be worried about you."

-CUT FAST ON, Bill looking into the peep hole through the cabin door and sees the eyes of Agents 2 and 3.5 standing right outside the door.

BILL/METROLINK TRAIN ANNOUNCER/OPERATOR

(Scared)

"Agents, Holy, Jesus, Marian Joseph.

DOCUMENTED FILE# 0000178

Ol' lord. I do not want to die...

Ol' lord, save me now....."

[Transmission-feed break]

-LOW WIDE ANGLE ON, Both agents banging on

the door trying to get into the operators

cabin. They are putting dents into the

metal but cannot penetrate the door.

BILL/METROLINK TRAIN ANNOUNCER/OPERATOR

"These agents will get in here

in no time. They are re-enforced with

level 10 bomb protection, but they are

too strong. What are we going to do,

they will kill me along

with you! Ol' Lord!"

DOCUMENTED FILE# 0000179

-RESUME WIDE ON, MICHEAL tapping his hand against Bill's shoulder. One of the agents breaks the side door of the train and flips up on top of the Metro link, walking towards the front of the train..

MICHEAL

"Shit, there on top of the train, they will find another way in sooner or later.."

BILL/METROLINK TRAIN ANNOUNCER/OPERATOR

"Just shut up, let me think"

MICHEAL

"We don't have time to think old man, look.."

DOCUMENTED FILE# 0000180

-WHIP PANNING ON, Agent #3.5 using a diamond cutter to cut a hole through the operator's window. Then Agent #3.5's arm transforms into a dead mini-gun and begins to shoot in MICHEAL's direction. MICHEAL begins shooting back...

BILL/METROLINK TRAIN ANNOUNCER/OPERATOR

"LOOK OUT..."

-TIGHT ON, Bill pushing MICHEAL out the way while some of the bullets hit Bill directly in the chest. While Agent #3.5 reloads. The Agent #2 starts to break through the operators cabin door. MICHEAL leans against the door..

BILL/METROLINK TRAIN ANNOUNCER/OPERATOR

"Arrgghhhhh, I'm hit....

Don't, don't wait

press the square button

and pull down that

shaft right next to you,

our cab will.."

-TIGHT ON, Bill passing out for a moment while MICHEAL presses the square gray button and pulls the shaft down. A rocket flares a bottom of the cab sending it shooting through the air, wings spread out, the cab turns into a small emergency aircraft.

PAN ON, Agent 3.5 falling off the cab below. MICHEAL rips out the control destination beacon and takes control of the cab heading towards Henry Blades' House on

Desert Drive. Bill is dying slowly. With his last few words Bill begins to talk to MICHEAL.

BILL/METROLINK TRAIN ANNOUNCER/OPERATOR

"Take my gun, it will help you get a couple of those bastards, I have extra shells in the storage area to the left. Whatever you did wrong, make sure you make it right, promise me that, take this map of the Circle District, it should help"

MICHEAL

(remorseful)

"I promise old man.

Thank you for

DOCUMENTED FILE# 0000183

saving my life

I will make sure of it,

if it's the last thing I do..."

[Transmission-feed break]

BILL/METROLINK TRAIN ANNOUNCER/OPERATOR

"Go, get, get out here..."

-PANNING DOWN ON, Bill passing away in MICHEAL's arms. MICHEAL closes the Bill's eyelids and covers his face with his jacket. MICHEAL looks over into the storage compartment and grabs the shotgun shells, jumps out of the Cabin looking for the area of Henry Blades Complex....

DOCUMENTED FILE# 0000184

(CUT TO:)

78. EXT. DESERT DRIVE - NIGHT

-LOW PANAGLIDE ON, MICHEAL walking to Desert Drive in the middle of the Desert. MICHEAL starts walking though the desert looking for Henry's location and cant pinpoint his exact location. MICHEAL stops near a section with a small dirt hill and take a breather to think. He looks right about 300 yards and notices a blue light blinking coming from the distance.

MICHEAL

(Whispering to himself)

"What's that blinking light over there?"

DOCUMENTED FILE# 0000185

-CAMERA TRACKS ON, MICHEAL walking closer to the blinking light, he walks up to a metal staff sticking out of a Box Plate screwed into the ground. He wipes the sand of the top of it, tripping the motion detector hearing a faint warning speaker. MICHEAL looks around not knowing what to expect next.

HENRY BLADES SECURITY SYSTEM VOICE

[Audio Voice]

"Security systems are activated.
These premises are off limits.
Get back, Deadly force
will be used if you
do not identify yourself as
known affiliate within the
next ten seconds"

DOCUMENTED FILE# 0000186

-PANAGLIDE ON, MICHEAL screaming out his name to the security system. Four Machine guns rise out of the sand surrounding MICHEAL and adjust their angles towards him.

[Transmission-feed break]

MICHEAL

(Screaming)

"Last name...Logan,

First Name.

MICHEAL, Identification Number 1180.."

HENRY BLADES SECURITY SYSTEM VOICE

[Audio Voice]

"Voice Analyzing, MICHEAL W. Logan

DOCUMENTED FILE# 0000187

Identification, one, one,

eight, zero"

Permission granted, proceed to

lower level. Proceed"

-PANNING DOWN ON, The metal box sliding back into the ground. Nothing happens right away. MICHEAL looks around in the darkness wondering what's going on.

The ground begins to rumble while a platform lifts up and a ramp slides down into a lower level.

MICHEAL walks down into dark platform area noticing a Lower Level" Sign illuminated. The Backup lights turn red and starts blinking faster and faster while the top of the platform comes down.

DOCUMENTED FILE# 0000188

BLACKOUT

79. INT. ENTRANCE LEVEL - HENRY BLADES COMPLEX - NIGHT

-FULL SHOT OF DARK SCREEN, A voice that sounds very familiar begins to speak towards MICHEAL asking him various questions, while a red light flicks slowly on and off...

HENRY BLADES-(MICHEAL's childhood friend)

[Audio Voice]

"MICHEAL, Logan is that you???
I thought you were... Dead?
Your all over the news for
assassinating Xavier"

MICHEAL [Audio Voice]

DOCUMENTED FILE# 0000189

(Joking)

"Well I didn't do it,

He was trying to kill me.

By the way what a nice Black Room

you have here, are you going to let

me in or are we playing hide and seek"

HENRY BLADES-(MICHEAL's childhood friend)

"Yeah, that's old MICHEAL alright

Come on into the complex,

Natasha will guide you..

MICHEAL

(talking to himself shaking his head)

"NATASHA?"

-LOW PANAGLIDE ON, white light appearing

in front of MICHEAL. Twin doors open up,

DOCUMENTED FILE# 0000190

MICHEAL walks through them and notices a passageway filled with pictures of the original Gateway Arch through the hall. -PANNING UP ON, MICHEAL looking up at the end of the hall and noticing a pair of sexy long legs with a face that he could never forget..

NATASHA-CYBERNETIC ROBOT/EXT TEAM

(Robotic sounding voice

with Czech Accent)

"Greetings, Mr. Logan, My name is Natasha. Mr. Blades is waiting for you in the engineering room.."

-TIGHT ON, MICHEAL touching the face of Natasha looking surprised because it's been re-programmed.

DOCUMENTED FILE# 0000191

MICHEAL

(shocked)

"You're a re-programmed Portal X
Facility Agent Number #2"

NATASHA-CYBERNETIC ROBOT/EXT TEAM

(Robotic sounding voice
with Czech Accent)

"Correct, Mr. Logan,
Mr. Blades programmed me
with past and present
memory data."

MICHEAL

(Replying)

"Impressive"

(CUT TO:)

DOCUMENTED FILE# 0000192

80. INT. ENGINEERING ROOM - HENRY BLADES COMPLEX - NIGHT

-LOW WIDE ANGLE ON, Natasha opening the doors to the engineering room filled with all different types of artillery. MICHEAL sees Blades wiping the dust off a wing to a Portal X Stealth Fighter Helicopter. MICHEAL begins to speak..

MICHEAL

(Replying)

"Where and the hell
did you get one of these?"

HENRY BLADES-(MICHEAL's childhood friend)

"You know me MICHEAL,
I always get the new toys

before the other black

market playboys get them"

MICHEAL

(Reminiscing)

"Yeah I remember when you made

the kids at The Facility school

freak out when you bought lunch for

all the girls in our class..

The administration thought you stole

money or something, remember that?"

HENRY BLADES-(MICHEAL's childhood friend)

"I earned that money fixing my father's

cars. I even drove them a couple times,

the girls loved it. Those where the good

old days"

DOCUMENTED FILE# 0000194

MICHEAL

(Questioning)

"How did you get a #2 agent

and a fighter copter?"

HENRY BLADES-(MICHEAL's childhood friend)

"I bought them from Xavier

not too long ago,

matter of fact he

owes me some missiles

for this little deal as well.

He wanted to me to find some

classified blueprints. I thought

if he wanted them so bad,

I needed some expensive equipment,

he knew they must have been important..

But I didn't give him this though,

I kept a small part of through the

DOCUMENTED FILE# 0000195

blueprints and there were wired money
account transfers from the Gov't to a
area in Northern Africa.
The details of some gateway being
constructed in Egypt."

MICHEAL

"Another Arch, do you mean
another Portal?.
In Egypt?"

HENRY BLADES-(MICHEAL's childhood friend)

"I don't know exactly.
The documents just
said it was delivered by
the Government to a
secret location inside
a Egyptian Pyramid.

DOCUMENTED FILE# 0000196

It was so Top Secret

that government where

treating it like

Area 51 or something"

MICHEAL

(Anxious)

"Well we got to there fast,

a friend of mine named

Jennifer is kidnapped

by the President and

he is planning to send a

biological weapon back

to earth to destroy

all human life on earth....

He's on Planet X as we speak..."

HENRY BLADES-(MICHEAL's childhood friend)

DOCUMENTED FILE# 0000197

"Planet X, There no such thing.

It's a myth everyone knows

it does not exist.

It's a old scientist tale and

by the way who is Jennifer?"

MICHEAL

(Anxious)

"I will tell you on the way let's go"

-HIGH WIDE SHOT ON, MICHEAL pulling Henry

aboard the helicopter. Henry tells Natasha

to jump aboard and begins to whistle for

his other 2 members to ride with them.

Red Falcon and King Nitro. Red Falcon

grabs all of his specialty weapons and

hops aboard. King Nitro straps his vest

on, locks and loads his guns, jumping

onto the helicopter. ANGLE REVERSE ON, the helicopter heading out of the engineering room. AERIAL VIEW, on the doors opening up above the surface. Sand begins to fall into the room and they rise up hovering above ground, the jet missiles fire up and once more and they blast off towards Egypt..

(CUT TO:)

80. INT. FLYING OVER THE ATLANTIC OCEAN -HELICOPTER - SUNRISE

AERIAL SHOT, While they're flying over the Atlantic Ocean, Henry looks out towards the sunrise and begins to start another conversation with MICHEAL about what's

going on.

HENRY BLADES-(MICHEAL's childhood friend)

"So what does this arch do?

And where the hell is Planet X?

MICHEAL

"Well I figured out that the

Gateway Arch is really a portal

to Planet X, using this metal

hypersonic pen device I found in

the Mediterranean sea. Planet X is in

a system not to far

from our solar system.

Me and Jennifer went through

another portal built by Xavier.

He acted like he

was going to kill

DOCUMENTED FILE# 0000200

the President but he

ended up killing Xavier Streets

instead. He kicked me

back through the Gateway to the

Portal X Facility in St. Louis City.

That's why I am here now.

The President wants to start

a new world and

rinse this one. He has

truly lost it, he promised

Xavier that he would rule

Earth after he delivers me to him.

To cut a long story short, I wanted to

let the world know they could have a

chance to live this discovery. To be

able to live on Planet X, the President

couldn't believe it wasn't the planet

Nibiru, which his staff first believed."

DOCUMENTED FILE# 0000201

HENRY BLADES-(MICHEAL's childhood friend)

"Sounds like if we don't

hurry up, doomsday will

be here before we know it.

Anyway, so how did

you meet this cop Jennifer?"

MICHEAL

"Another long story, She

arrested me while I was

sitting in this car on

the landing in St. Louis,

my memory was erased, but somehow

it ended up coming back"

HENRY BLADES-(MICHEAL's childhood friend)

"Arrested? Your mind erased?

Did you hear that Natasha?"

DOCUMENTED FILE# 0000202

[Transmission-feed break]

-TIGHT ON HENRY, Tapping Natasha on her thigh.

HENRY BLADES-(MICHEAL's childhood friend)

(Continuing)

"Sounds like the President

is really taking

this God thing

to his head."

-LOW WIDE ANGLE ON, Henry rallying up his EXTeam while inside the helicopter. TIGHT ON, Henry and MICHEAL filling them in for attack, while they look at the blueprints and various maps of Egypt..

The computerized helicopter driver

DOCUMENTED FILE# 0000203

operator speaks through the intercom to the rest of the team…

HENRY'S EXTEAM HELICOPTER OPERATOR C5

(V.O.)

(Computerized)

"We are approaching our certified

location. ETA. 16 minutes.

Destination Cairo.."

HENRY BLADES-(MICHEAL's childhood friend)

"Alright EXTeam, let's look over the

blueprint plans for entering

The Portal X inside of

the Great Pyramid one more time.

As most know, it was

built by Pharaoh Khufu.

Its 480.97 ft. High.

The Pyramid has three
burial chambers.
The first is underground carved in
bedrock. The second is above ground.
The 3rd is the King's Chamber.
It had a red Granite sarcophagus
inside but was take out
to build the The Arch...
We will enter the king's chamber
through the twenty-six foot high
grand gallery. There are
sliding granite blocking
systems that are
now state of the art,
this will lead us to
the actual portal.
This is a smallest version ever
built. Approx. 23 feet high.

DOCUMENTED FILE# 0000205

We have to take our dune buggies down to the East Side of the pyramid. There are security posts on the east and west corner. The watchtower on top of the pyramid has a 360-degrees motion sensor that are state of the art. There's also sixteen hot spots inside the pyramid using heat scanning systems, so we will have to use our cooling body suits to stay off the scanning grid"

[Transmission-feed break]

DOCUMENTED FILE# 0000206

MICHEAL

(Curious)

"There are too many risks entering

the King's Chamber?"

HENRY BLADES-(MICHEAL's childhood

friend)

"Well there's a shaft that was drilled

out leading to the Queen's Chamber.

There's a keypad locking system that The

President and the Secretary the Defense

knows, so once we enter it, they will

know it has been breached.

But its out best shot"

HENRY'S EXTEAM HELICOPTER OPERATOR C5

(V.O.)

DOCUMENTED FILE# 0000207

(Computerized)

"ETA 2 minutes.."

HENRY BLADES-(MICHEAL's childhood friend)

"Alright boys its lock and load time,
get ready to roll EXTeam, this isn't
some transformers, so lock sharp OORAH!"
[HENRY using his Marines chant]

(CUT TO:)

81. EXT. THE DESERT - CAIRO, EGYPT - NIGHT

-AERIAL SHOT ON, MICHEAL, Henry and his EXTeam (Natasha, Red Falcon and King Nitro) jumping out the Helicopter with their buggies. They begin driving to the Great Pyramid. FULL SHOT ON, The whole team 300 yards from the pyramid. Natasha shoots

both guards with her sniper rifle on the East and West side from long distance...

They all jump off their buggies and start climbing up the pyramid avoiding the motion tower on the top. They enter the shaft vault entrance to the keypad. TIGHT ON, Red Falcon trying to break the lock while Henry notices that the tower motion detector light projector is turning their way..

HENRY BLADES-(MICHEAL's childhood friend)

"Red Falcon get us in. now.."

RED FALCON/Henry Blades EXTeam

(Replying)

"I'm on it, I'm on It."

-SEQUENCE OF SHOTS, as the motion light is turning around the base of the pyramid using a red spotlight. WHIP PANNING ON, Red Falcon rushing to get the team in. TIGHT ON, Red Falcon pressing a melody sequence. ON-SCREEN SHOT, on the numbers rolling down until the lock reads open, and unlocks.

                                        (CUT TO:)

82. INT. SHAFT|QUEEN'S CHAMBER - THE GREAT PYRAMID - NIGHT

-PANNING DOWN, on everyone climbing in the entrance part of the shaft. Before they reach the end of the shaft, King Nitro notices fiber optic cables inside the

DOCUMENTED FILE# 0000210

shaft with orange lasers scanning every inch of the shaft…

[Transmission-feed break]

RED FALCON/Henry Blades EXTeam

"Wait a minute, these lasers are 3x times hotter then the sun. It will take me a while to get pass this breaker security system."

-WHIP PANNING ON, Red Falcon looking back at Nitro

(CUT TO:)

RED FALCON/Henry Blades EXTeam

"King I need you"

DOCUMENTED FILE# 0000211

HENRY BLADES-(MICHEAL's childhood friend)

"Let's go, where running out

of time, come on."

KING NITRO/Henry Blades EXTeam

(Replying)

"Yes sir"

-TIGHT ON, King Nitro pulling out a sliding rectangle device that redirects the laser into the device to pass by. Nitro places part of the device into place. Then King presses the 2nd button on the side of his arm control device and actives the rectangle device.

KING NITRO/Henry Blades EXTeam

"This is the strongest metal

in the world. Resistance to

8 times the temperature of

the sun. We have to

wait for the lights to blink

in three-second time frames.

Then It will blink 5 times.

After the 5th time someone has

to slide though. Let's go."

(CUT TO:)

83. INT. QUEEN'S CHAMBER - THE GREAT PYRAMID - NIGHT

-REVERSE ANGLE ON, Each EXTeam member

one by one waiting for the sequence and

sliding into the Queen's Chamber. TIGHT

DOCUMENTED FILE# 0000213

ON, Red Falcon sliding down the shaft, barely making it through, he nicks his backpack on the lasers as they retract back but he safely slides through..

KING NITRO/Henry Blades EXTeam

"Whoa look at your bag.."

RED FALCON/Henry Blades EXTeam

"Holy shit, I'm still on fire.."

HENRY BLADES-(MICHEAL's childhood friend)

(Amazed)

"Shhhh, look"

-PANAGLIDE ON, everyone looking around as they see hieroglyphics on the wall and noticing the exit that will take them

DOCUMENTED FILE# 0000214

into the King's Chamber. TIGHT ON, MICHEAL
stepping on stone activating a trap stone.
WHIP PANNING ON, Natasha pulling MICHEAL
from under the doorway as a large stone
slides down almost smashing on him.
REVERSE ANGLE ON, King Nitro stepping in
front of the stone wall adding his C-4 kit
to take out the barricade.

HENRY BLADES-(MICHEAL's childhood friend)

"Get the hell out the

way, King hit it.."

-TIGHT ON, Nitro aiming towards the door.
He presses his detonator and blows up the
stone at a low sound level.

DOCUMENTED FILE# 0000215

HENRY BLADES-(MICHEAL's childhood friend)

"BOOM.."

-SEQUENCE OF SHOTS ON, Nitro clearing the debris in front of the doorways. He notices two agents running towards the Queens Chamber shooting in their direction..

HENRY BLADES-(MICHEAL's childhood friend)

"Get in attack position"

-CUT FAST ON, Henry pulling out his automatic weapon shooting towards agents. TIGHT ON, both agents flipping out of the way. Natasha pulls out her two Uzis and shoots them down in their tracks. Natasha looks at Henry and says:

DOCUMENTED FILE# 0000216

NATASHA-CYBERNETIC ROBOT/EXT TEAM

"Losing your touch"

-TIGHT ON, Natasha blowing the smoke off both smoking gun barrels. MICHEAL begins to talk with Henry.

MICHEAL

"If I'm correct the Kings
Chamber is right over here"

(CUT TO:)

84. INT. PASSAGEWAY - THE GREAT PYRAMID - NIGHT

-PANAGLIDE ON, The entire team walking into the passageway noticing that it has

DOCUMENTED FILE# 0000217

been renovated. They begin walking down a small ramp which opens up to the twenty-six foot entranceway to the King's Chamber. -TIGHT ON, The whole team pausing for a second.....

RED FALCON/Henry Blades EXTeam

(Talking quietly)

"Wow look at this gallery,

it's still intact after

all these years.."

HENRY BLADES-(MICHEAL's childhood friend)

"Let's get focused, more

agents could be ahead"

(CUT TO:)

DOCUMENTED FILE# 0000218

85. EXT. THE DESERT - CAIRO, EGYPT - NIGHT

AERIAL SHOT ON, Two government fully armed Portal X Facility Helicopter Jets heading towards the Great Pyramid's location.

(CUT TO:)

86. INT. KING'S CHAMBER - THE GREAT PYRAMID - NIGHT

-FULL SHOT on The EXTeam walk into the King's chamber they notice something that makes them a bit puzzled.

-TIGHT ON, Natasha noticing some maps that once of the agents where carrying and picks them up.

DOCUMENTED FILE# 0000219

MICHEAL

"Where is the portal?

I was wondering why there

weren't many

agents here. The President

must of moved it from this location."

KING NITRO/Henry Blades EXTeam

"So what do we do now?"

-TIGHT|ON SCREEN, Red Falcon's Monitoring

Systems device starts blinking. He notices

the helicopter jets heading their way..

RED FALCON/Henry Blades EXTeam

(Worried)

"We got a serious problem. Two bogeys

Are coming our way, ETA 7 minutes"

DOCUMENTED FILE# 0000220

(CUT TO)

86. EXT. ENTRANCE - THE GREAT PYRAMID - NIGHT

-ANGLE, FOLLOW The EXTeam quickly running back to their buggies and heading towards their buggies.

HENRY BLADES-(MICHEAL's childhood friend)

"Natasha look back through those maps that you found on that agent. Look and see if you can find something. Henry, radio the Helicopter to swoop us up at a closer."

BLACKOUT

DOCUMENTED FILE# 0000221

(CUT TO:)

86. EXT. HELICOPTER CHASE - THE DESERT - NIGHT

-WIDE ANGLE ON, The EXTeam racing back to meet up with their copter at the rendezvous point, both Gov't Helicopter's open fire on the EXTeam buggies. AERIAL SHOT ON, both Government Helicopters shooting in the direction of the EXTeam, the bullets are hitting the sand almost hitting them as the EXTeam dodges out of the way. REVERSE ANGLE ON, Henry noticing MICHEAL's buggie malfunctioning because his gas tank is loosing gas from bullet hit. Henry slows down to help him. TIGHT ON, MICHEAL looking back at the approaching helicopters,

gripping his handle bars. MICHEAL jumps onto Henry's helicopter. Henry radio's in to his helicopter operator…

HENRY BLADES-(MICHEAL's childhood friend)

(Yelling)

"Code Red. We need extraction now, get your ass over here now!"

HENRY'S EXTEAM HELICOPTER OPERATOR C5

(V.O.)

(Computerized)

"Copy leader, 100 yards away. Located sand storm formations coming your way"

-WHIP PANNING ON, Government Agents inside of the helicopters unloading their

DOCUMENTED FILE# 0000223

machine guns shooting while the EXTeam
dodges the incoming fire. MICHEAL notices
a huge sand dune in the same direction of
a sand storm.

MICHEAL

"Let's head towards that huge sand dune
over there, it will help us get some
cover so we can loose them in the sand
storm is coming.."

RED FALCON/Henry Blades EXTeam

(Questioning)

"Are you crazy? You'll lead us
directly into the sand storm"

[Transmission-feed break]

DOCUMENTED FILE# 0000224

KING NITRO/Henry Blades EXTeam

"That's suicide"

MICHEAL

"You got a better idea"

-TIGHT ON, Henry getting his team into order, knowing that MICHEAL's plan can be risky. He calls upon Nitro, the trustworthy gun soldier.

HENRY BLADES-(MICHEAL's childhood friend)

(Yelling)

"We are rolling with MICHEAL's plan. Nitro, give us some time to get to the helicopter, may god be with You we will meet you at rally point 2. Split up on my lead, NOW, BREAK WAY!"

DOCUMENTED FILE# 0000225

-SEQUENCE OF SHOTS ON, MICHEAL and The EXTeam breaking up heading towards the sand storm while Nitro stands guard near the sand formation to take care of the Government helicopters.

KING NITRO/Henry Blades EXTeam

"Yes Sir"

HENRY BLADES-(MICHEAL's childhood friend)

"Operator, proceed to rally point 2. ETA ASAP, Over."

HENRY'S EXTEAM HELICOPTER OPERATOR C5

(V.O.)

(Computerized)

"Roger that, Flight plan changed to Rally Point 2"

-PANNING UP, on the EXTeam helicopter, changing direction to the shores of the Mediterranean Sea.

-WHIP PANNING ON, Nitro moving towards the government helicopters he starts shooting rapidly at one of the copters. He hits the tail of the copter leaving the copter falling towards the ground in a 360 motion smashing on the sand dune. The pilot of the government helicopter releases his escape pods, which turn into mini aircrafts.

-TIGHT ON, Nitro raising his eyebrows in amazement as they are heading towards him. The other helicopter flies through the smoke of the wreckage, into the sand storm. The 5 pods start chasing Nitro

shooting him down, killing him instantly before he enters the sand storm.

HENRY BLADES-(MICHEAL's childhood friend)

(Screaming)

"Nitroooo.….."

-TIGHT ON, The EXTeam notices that Nitro lifeline went flat line on their data systems. They begin putting rags and goggles over their faces entering the sand storm.

(CUT TO:)

87. EXT. SANDSTORM - THE DESERT - NIGHT

-FULL SHOT ON , The government helicopter

searching for MICHEAL and the EXTeam. Henry notices the 5 pods closing in on their location, he sneaks around and shoots them all down one by one. Red Falcon begin to talk to Henry over the radio about the last helicopter…

RED FALCON/Henry Blades EXTeam

[Audio Voice]

"We must shoot that last copter, they have a lock on our position"

....

[Transmission-feed break/error/re/online]

-WHIP PANNING, on C5 the EXTeam helicopter

DOCUMENTED FILE# 0000229

operator, not obeying orders to meet them at Rally Point 2. C5 finds them in the sand storm saving them. Everyone quickly ride their buggies into the helicopter while they all look at each other with relief. The helicopter exit's the sand storm heading towards Cairo as the last government helicopter is tailing them..

(CUT TO:)

88. INT. HELICOPTER - THE DESERT - NIGHT

HENRY BLADES-(MICHEAL's childhood friend)

"Natasha you're up next,

EXTeam in formation."

NATASHA-CYBERNETIC ROBOT/EXT TEAM

DOCUMENTED FILE# 0000230

"I'm two steps in head of you.

C5 take me in"

HENRY'S EXTEAM HELICOPTER OPERATOR C5

(V.O.)

(Computerized)

"Roger"

-PANNING UP ON, Jennifer jumping out the helicopter with her arms stretched out wide and her legs straight. Natasha swoops down as she swings underneath the helicopter shooting down the last government helicopter with her Uzis making it crash and burn. TIGHT ON, MICHEAL looking on with amazement. CUT FAST ON, C5 noticing they are running out of fuel from being a bullet shots into the gas tank.

DOCUMENTED FILE# 0000231

HENRY'S EXTEAM HELICOPTER OPERATOR C5

(V.O.)

(Computerized)

"Damage to fuel shell, fuel

capacity is now down to 15% percent.

There are 5 percent reserves are still

remaining. We need to land fast.

-CLOSE ON, everyone looking at Henry for

his response, before he speaks Red Falcon.

Henry begins to speak reckless slamming

his foot down on the floor.

RED FALCON/Henry Blades EXTeam

"Nitro is dead Sir, I vowed

never to turn my back

on your judgment. I loved

Nitro as if he was my

DOCUMENTED FILE# 0000232

brother, its time to

tell MICHEAL the truth.

About the 4th portal.

Natasha pulls her gun out

on Red Falcon thinking

that he has lost it."

MICHEAL

"WHAT? There's a 4th portal?"

NATASHA-CYBERNETIC ROBOT/EXT TEAM

"Stand down soldier, what are you

doing?"

HENRY BLADES-(MICHEAL's childhood friend)

"No Natasha, No, god damn it

stand down, stand down now.

Don't break up on me soldiers,

DOCUMENTED FILE# 0000233

we need to land this bird and

figure out what's next after

we repair this bird."

HENRY'S EXTEAM HELICOPTER OPERATOR C5

(V.O.)

(Computerized)

"Fuel Capacity now on reserves"

-ANGLE, on MICHEAL looks at Henry with

disgust, Henry looks away and puts his

head down as his bandanna swirls around

his head...

(CUT TO:)

89. EXT. RALLY POINT 2 - NILE RIVER|CAIRO

- MORNING

-PULL BACK ON, The EXTeam stopping for repairs. MICHEAL walks along the Nile River washing his hands in the water. SEQUENCE OF SHOTS ON, Red Falcon and Natasha fixing the helicopter, while Henry is walking over to MICHEAL to begin explaining about the 4th portal… MICHEAL looks at Henry with disappointment before Henry starts talking.

HENRY BLADES-(MICHEAL's childhood friend)

"What I do know is that, The President was rumored to spend large amounts of money into land north of the Nile river..

Only The President is authorized to use this facility. Security checks out the ass, if you know what I mean. It's

DOCUMENTED FILE# 0000235

somewhere near the north coast of Africa and the Mediterranean Sea. This facility is supposed to be different from the other two, it was built under water. It can lead directly towards Planet X by using the portal or by using an aircraft with the same technology but by moving through space."

MICHEAL

"Wait I found that hypersonic pen object right around the same area, if what you telling me is true. They have found out the true technology   and where it has come from originally, We got to get there. Where is the map again?"

-TIGHT SHOT ON, MAP OF THE MEDITERRANEAN

DOCUMENTED FILE# 0000236

SEA, HIGH WIDE SHOT, Red Falcon and Natasha fixing the helicopter waving to Henry pointing towards the bird that it has been completely repaired.

MICHEAL

"Okay, by the look of the map,

the portal's location is

in the deepest part of the sea.

Located in the Calypso Deep

in the Ionian Sea.

That is the deepest part

of the Mediterranean Sea,

so it makes since why they

would build it there."

[Transmission-feed break]

DOCUMENTED FILE# 0000237

HENRY BLADES-(MICHEAL's childhood friend)

"I don't know why I didn't tell you before I guess the greed in me wanted to find it myself"

MICHEAL

"Well make it up by getting us there"

(CUT TO:)

90. INT. PRESIDENT'S QUARTERS - PLANET X FACILITY- NIGHT

-PANNING UP, INSIDE OF THE PRESIDENT'S QUARTERS The entrance door opens up with a high-pitch mechanical sound.

DOCUMENTED FILE# 0000238

THE PRESIDENT OF THE UNITED STATES

"Welcome to our new home Jennifer,

(he chuckles) Guards leave us"

[Transmission-feed break]

JENNIFER/Female Police Officer

"I will never obey to what you say"

THE PRESIDENT OF THE UNITED STATES

(Sarcastic)

"Ha, Jennider, Jennifer,

Jennifer, Jennifer"

JENNIFER/Female Police Officer

"What's so freaking funny?"

DOCUMENTED FILE# 0000239

THE PRESIDENT OF THE UNITED STATES

"How can you not see my plan?

We will become gods.

I will be know as the creator

of all human life.

You will carry my baby and

I will take care of

you my queen (seductive).

So why are you worried

about the people on Earth?

Aids has completely taken over,

People have destroy our

world with pollution like

never before. So tell me,

what or who is worth saving?"

JENNIFER/Female Police Officer

"Worth saving, the corporations

DOCUMENTED FILE# 0000240

have done the most damage,

when I was a kid, I flew in

a plane and looked over the

city and it was so clear,

so beautiful.

When I grew up 20 years later,

I took the same trip and

looked outside the window

and I saw pollution in

the air that I never saw before.

Usually you would only

see that over major cities

like California or New York City,

now you see pollution even

over the small cities"

THE PRESIDENT OF THE UNITED STATES

"I like that in you Jennifer,

DOCUMENTED FILE# 0000241

such a heart for mankind.

I wish I could have a heart

like you do for the people.

I used to when I first

got into office, but now

we must begin"

(stopping abruptly)

-CAMERA TRACKS ON, two security agents

entering the President's quarters grabbing

Jennifer.

(CUT TO:)

91. INT. ALEXANDRIA - EGYPT - DAY

-AERIAL SHOT ON, the EXTeam flying over

Alexandria. MICHEAL looks out at the

sphinx smiling as they fly over the rest of the city from its beauty, thinking about Jennifer.

(CUT TO:)

90. INT. INFIRMARY - PLANET X FACILITY-NIGHT

-LOW ANGLE AS FOLLOW, the security agents and the President walking Jennifer into the Infirmary, The Doctors begins to unstrap the seat for Jennifer to get into. At the same time Jennifer quickly grabs one of the guards guns, shooting them in the face. The President begins to clap with amazement and begins to speak.

DOCUMENTED FILE# 0000243

THE PRESIDENT OF THE UNITED STATES

"Congrats, Jennifer. I see your police training has paid off. So what are you going to do now?"

JENNIFER/Female Police Officer

"I will kill you if you come. any closer, don't test me"

THE PRESIDENT OF THE UNITED STATES

"There's no way back to Earth, for I only have the access sequence"

-TIGHT ON, The president walking closer to Jennifer

JENNIFER/Female Police Officer

"Make one more step,

DOCUMENTED FILE# 0000244

I'm telling you

right now get back"

THE PRESIDENT OF THE UNITED STATES

(Replying with a deceiving voice)
"We are similar me and you, put the gun
down, think about what you're doing"

JENNIFER/Female Police Officer

"We are nothing alike. I don't want
anything from you, get back"

-WHIP PANNING, on an Air Duct to the left.
Jennifer starts walking towards it, aiming
her gun at everyone in the infirmary. One of
the doctors pressed the emergency button
which brings 3 more guards into the room...

DOCUMENTED FILE# 0000245

91. INT. INFIRMARY - PLANET X FACILITY-

NIGHT

THE PRESIDENT OF THE UNITED STATES

(Deceiving)

"What are you trying to do

Jennifer?, There's no escape.

I told you, choose your

destiny with me,

come to me"

-CUT FAST ON, Jennifer pulling the Air
Duct crate off and begins turning around
for one more look...

THE PRESIDENT OF THE UNITED STATES

(Deceiving)

"Jennifer, don't be afraid, guards,

DOCUMENTED FILE# 0000246

BRING HER TO ME ALIVE"

(CUT TO:)

91. INT. AIR DUCT SHAFT - PLANET X FACILITY- NIGHT

-WHIP PANNING, on Jennifer jumping in the air duct as she slides down going faster and faster not knowing where she is going. She begins to slow herself down by pushing her hands and feet against the side of the air duct shaft.

(CUT TO:)

92. INT. END OF AIR DUCT SHAFT - PLANET X FACILITY- NIGHT

DOCUMENTED FILE# 0000247

-ANGLE BETWEEN, The air duct shaft from a REVERSE ANGLE looking at Jennifer.

(CUT TO:)

93. INT. END OF AIR DUCT SHAFT - PLANET X FACILITY- NIGHT

-TIGHT ON, Jennifer noticing 2 guards walking by outside of the air duct.

(CUT TO:)

94. INT. AIRCRAFT HANGER - PLANET X FACILITY- NIGHT

-HIGH WIDE SHOT ON, The two guards listening to their radio, then start running out of

the hanger looking for Jennifer…

[Transmission-feed break/error/re/online]

(CUT TO:)

95. INT. END OF AIR DUCT SHAFT - PLANET X FACILITY- NIGHT

-TIGHT ON, Jennifer kicking the cover to the shaft off.

(CUT TO:)

96. INT. AIRCRAFT HANGER - PLANET X FACILITY- NIGHT

-CRANE SHOT, on Jennifer heading towards the 1st aircraft she sees, hopping

into it. She logs in destination Earth, knowing that this particular aircraft will not make it there. Jennifer sets up a trap, to make the President believe that she was flown out of the Facility. Jennifer jumps out of the aircraft hiding inside of a storage crate. The aircraft she sets on autopilot begins to fly out towards the exit. Alarms begin to sound. Two agents run into the hanger and begin shooting the aircraft blowing it up before it reaches outside the chamber...

(CUT TO:)

97. INT. PRESIDENT'S QUARTERS - PLANET X FACILITY- NIGHT

DOCUMENTED FILE# 0000250

-ON-SCREEN SHOT, on the president looking at the aircraft blowing up outside the facility. The President radios the guards.

THE PRESIDENT OF THE UNITED STATES

[Audio Voice]

"You fools I told you to

capture her not kill her,

Now I will need another

woman for the process.

God damn it!"

(CUT TO:)

97. INT. AIRCRAFT HANGER - PLANET X

FACILITY- NIGHT

DOCUMENTED FILE# 0000251

-TIGHT ON, the President walking into the aircraft hanger. The president pulls out a small weapon and shoots down the agent he believed to have shot the aircraft. He looks over at the other agent and begins to speak.

THE PRESIDENT OF THE UNITED STATES
"This will happen to anyone
to you as well, if you do not
follow my orders.
I am going to sleep for
a while, do not disturb
me until you come back
from Earth with my replacement,
and make sure she is a virgin"

[Transmission-feed break/reboot/online]

DOCUMENTED FILE# 0000252

98. INT. PRESIDENT'S QUARTERS - PLANET X FACILITY- NIGHT

-PAN, on the President walking into his quarters. As the agent takes one of the aircrafts with light speed to make it to earth to find another replacement… .

99. INT. AIRCRAFT HANGER - PLANET X FACILITY- NIGHT

-LOW WIDE ANGLE, on another guard dragging the body of the dead agent out into garbage disposal.

(CUT TO:)

100. INT. STORAGE CRATE - PLANET X FACILITY - NIGHT

-TIGHT ON, Jennifer watching the whole thing, shes quietly waiting for all the guards to leave.

(CUT TO:)

101. INT. DARK HALLWAY - PLANET X FACILITY- NIGHT

-ANGLE- FOLLOW, Jennifer walking out of the hanger into a dark hallway with green neon lights along the floor. More instrumentation making sounds, on and off. Jennifer continues to walk down the hallway trying to find a way off Planet X.

(CUT TO:)

DOCUMENTED FILE# 0000254

102. INT CALYPSO DEEP - IONIAN SEA - LATE AFTERNOON

-AERIAL SHOT, on the EXTeam hovering above the water, everyone hops into a portable mini sub-marine and proceeds to the Portal X Facility underwater.

103. EXT. MINI-SUB MARINE - CALYPSO DEEP -LATE AFTERNOON

-FOLLOW, the mini-sub going deeper into the water, noticing a glass dome built underneath the water.

(CUT TO:)

DOCUMENTED FILE# 0000255

104. INT. DECOMPRESSION ROOM - PORTAL FACILITY- NIGHT

-ANGLE, on The EXTeam, heading into the dome, entering the pressure locking system to decompress.

(CUT TO:)

105. INT. IONIAN SEA PORTAL FACILITY- NIGHT

MICHEAL

"Would you look at that"

-HIGH WIDE SHOT, on the EXTeam looking at a futuristic spaceship. There are no guards around which makes everyone a

little suspicious because they also notice that there is no portal as well. Without wasting anytime, everyone hops into the aircraft to ship…

(CUT TO:)

106. INT. PORTAL AIRCRAFT - NIGHT

HENRY BLADES-(MICHEAL's childhood friend)

"Natasha can fly this thing,

by the looks of it, there are

light speed capabilities"

-TIGHT ON, Henry with Natasha begin pressing all the controls on the aircraft switchboard for immediate start up.

[Transmission-feed break]

DOCUMENTED FILE# 0000257

107. EXT. PORTAL AIRCRAFT - IONIAN SEA - NIGHT

-FULL SHOT, on the aircraft lifting up, flying out the exit where a force field keeps the water from coming in..

Within seconds the aircraft disappear with a bust of light in the atmosphere...

(CUT TO:)

108. EXT. ITALY - NIGHT

-FULL SHOT, on a crowd of people on the beach looking at the aircraft leaving the light in the sky.

(CUT TO:)

109. EXT. SPACE - GALAXY

-ANGLE, on the aircraft passing the planets in our solar system. Everyone looking though the front windshield amazed at what they see..

[Transmission-feed break]

                                          (CUT TO:)

FADE IN

110. INT. PORTAL AIRCRAFT - SPACE

-ON-SCREEN SHOT, of MICHEAL looking at the middle on the console, noticing that they will reach Planet X in two hours and sixteen minutes. The aircraft goes into

DOCUMENTED FILE# 0000259

light speed faster than 61 million times
the speed of light across to a new galaxy.
111,000 light-years across...

                MICHEAL [Audio Voice]

            (thinking to himself)

        "Hold on Jennifer, Hold On"

**111. EXT. PORTAL AIRCRAFT - PX 11C
GALAXY SYSTEM**

FULL SHOT on the spaceship is flying
through space passing the stars and
nebula's approaching the galaxy PX 11C

**112. INT. CONTROL ROOM - PLANET X
FACILITY**

DOCUMENTED FILE# 0000260

-LOW WIDE ANGLE, on The Portal X Facility picking up The EXTeam spaceship approaching Planet X. The control guards immediately informs the president.

(CUT TO:)

113. INT. PRESIDENT'S QUARTERS - PLANET X FACILITY

-ON SCREEN SHOT, videophone ringing inside the President's Quarters. The President picks up with a fierce tone.

THE PRESIDENT OF THE UNITED STATES (O.S.)

"What, Didn't I tell you not to disturb me for any reason?"

(CUT TO:)

114. INT. CONTROL ROOM - PLANET X FACILITY

PORTAL X FACILITY CONTROL ROOM GUARD

(O.S.)

"Yes, Mr. President but we have intruders

heading towards our location from the

north east end of the planet,

what do you want us to do, Sir?"

THE PRESIDENT OF THE UNITED STATES (O.S.)

(Replying)

"Send two fighter planes to intercept,

NO WAIT, Let them land and bring

them to me alive, no screw ups"

DOCUMENTED FILE# 0000262

PORTAL X FACILITY CONTROL ROOM GUARD

(O.S.)

"Yes, Sir, command, you heard The President. Let them land and bring them alive with our X-Trackers.

(CUT TO:)

115. EXT. PORTAL X FACILITY SPACESHIP - PLANET X

-PULL BACK, on the spaceship approaching the atmosphere of Planet X.

116. INT. PORTAL X FACILITY SPACESHIP AIRCRAFT - PLANET X

DOCUMENTED FILE# 0000263

-ANGLE, on everyone inside of the ship looking surprised on how much Planet X looks earth-like. TIGHT ON, the ship reading the planet's temperature ON-SCREEN, --No Pollution -- 86 degrees -- Clear skies

HENRY BLADES-(MICHEAL's childhood friend)

(Intuition)

"Something doesn't smell right,

I can just feel it.

There's no way in hell they

would of let us come in

this far without sending

any attackers. Let's land

2 miles away from

the Planet X Facility

then move in"

DOCUMENTED FILE# 0000264

NATASHA-CYBERNETIC ROBOT/EXT TEAM

"We should pack some extra

fire power, Red, give MICHEAL

some extra gear"

117. INT. ARTILLERY STORAGE - PORTAL

AIRCRAFT - PLANET X

-TIGHT ON, MICHEAL picking up an auto-hand

gun with explosive shells. He also picks

up a state of the art vest that can block

most rounds including 50. Caliber.

(CUT TO:)

118. EXT. PORTAL AIRCRAFT - PLANET X -

NIGHT

-HIGH WIDE SHOT, on the spaceship landing on Planet X. The back ramp begins to decline slowly. The EXTeam walks out of the aircraft, noticing a distant moon in the horizon.

PANNING UP, on Henry noticing a nebula on the other side of the horizon making the planet appear with a blue glare (a neon light effect) Everything that is white, including their gear, eyes and teeth, are glowing in the dark from the neon blue nebula in the sky.

119. EXT. PLANET X - NIGHT

HENRY BLADES-(MICHEAL's childhood friend)
    "Well I guess we won't stick
    out like a sore thumb"

DOCUMENTED FILE# 0000266

MICHEAL

"Yeah tell me about it"

HENRY BLADES-(MICHEAL's childhood friend)

"Let's get these bastards.
Natasha, Red, MICHEAL, we will move
out in triangle
defensive formation."

(CUT TO:)

120. EXT. PLANET X CITY - PLANET X - NIGHT

-CRANE SHOT, on The EXTeam sneaking into the city. They notice that there are no sensors protecting the city.

DOCUMENTED FILE# 0000267

HENRY BLADES-(MICHEAL's childhood friend)

"This city looks like Las Vegas"

RED FALCON/Henry Blades EXTeam

"Yes but one small mistake

and the President will

know we are here."

-TIGHT ON, Red Falcon looking through the
city with his heat signal/motion sensor
binoculars...

RED FALCON/Henry Blades EXTeam

[Audio Voice]

(Anxious)

"Sir, let me be the distraction,

I will head to the left

side of the city to draw

DOCUMENTED FILE# 0000268

off the mobile gunners.
I bet you that they work
together in unison.
It's going to be tricky
to get rid of them but if
you head towards the
main gate of the facility
I will draw them off by light
heat flares"

HENRY BLADES-(MICHEAL's childhood friend)

(Honored)

"Red, I honor you decision,
time is running out so we will
move in near the side
entrances once we reach
inside of the main gate then
meet up with us back at the ship

DOCUMENTED FILE# 0000269

RED FALCON/Henry Blades EXTeam

"Yes Sir"

121. INT. CONTROL ROOM - PLANET X FACILITY - NIGHT

-ON-SCREEN, the Control room guard starts to actives the Planet X-Trackers and Planet X-Gunners. They all turn on transforming out from a small circle on the floor. The control guard programs them to move towards the most heat signals on the left side of the city. (X-Trackers can cocoon any target by spraying a hardening gel and bring them back to any location.)

-TIGHT ON, The Control Pressing the Main console, deploying the Planet X-Trackers

into the city towards Red Falcon.

THE PRESIDENT OF THE UNITED STATES (O.S.)

(on-screen inside the control room)

"Did they really think

they can come

and kill me in my world?

This is the 2nd

time and this will be their last.

Come into my trap EXTeam"

PLANET X FACILITY CONTROL ROOM GUARD

[Audio Voice]

"Not so fast Sir, we picked

up a total of four unknown

moving signals. Three signals

are moving towards the Facility,

DOCUMENTED FILE# 0000271

the last signal is coming

from inside of the facility."

(CUT TO:)

122. INT. PRESIDENT'S QUARTERS - PLANET X

FACILITY- NIGHT

THE PRESIDENT OF THE UNITED STATES

"What, Jennifer is still alive?"

(putting his hand on his chin)

"I will take care of her myself,

Track the rest of the EXTeam NOW!"

PLANET X FACILITY CONTROL ROOM GUARD

[Audio Voice]

"Yes Sir"

DOCUMENTED FILE# 0000272

(CUT TO:)

123. EXT. THE STRIP OF PLANET X CITY - PLANET X - NIGHT

-RESUME WIDE, on Red Falcon moving down the strip of the city. He notices a mobile gunner coming down the middle of the road. Red Falcon slides to the left behind a pillar of a building. He cannot spot the other gunner on his scanner but knows that it is somewhere around the area. TIGHT ON, the 1st gunner moving down the street, stopping in the middle of the road, facing towards the pillar where Red Falcon is hiding. Red Falcon cocks his machine guns back and gets ready to be attacked.

DOCUMENTED FILE# 0000273

RED FALCON/Henry Blades EXTeam

"Where in the hell is the 2nd gunner,

I can't expose myself

without knowing

It's Location. Damn It"

-LOW WIDE ANGLE, on Red Falcon looking at his scanner noticing that the 2nd mobile gunner is entering the building right behind him.

SPLIT-SCREEN/SEQUENCE OF SHOTS The 2nd gunner shoots a heat-seeking missile towards Red Falcon. The 1st gunner doesn't move from its position. WHIP PANNING, on Red Falcon jumping out from behind the pillar and begins to run towards the

direction of the 1st gunner.

RED FALCON/Henry Blades EXTeam

"If I'm going out,

I am taking both

of ya'll with me…"

124. EXT. SIDEWALK - THE STRIP OF PLANET X CITY - NIGHT

-CUT FAST, on Red Falcon approaching the 1st gunner with only seconds to spare. Red Falcon does a double front flip while the missile destroys the 1st gunner. TIGHT ON, a piece of debris hitting Red Falcon in his back wounding him badly. Red Falcon turns around for a short second and noticed that the 2nd Gunner is right behind him. Red Falcon takes out a nuclear grenade and pressing the activation code for detonation, within seconds the blast destroys everything in 20 yards.

(CUT TO:)

125. EXT. MAIN GATE OF PLANET X FACILITY - NIGHT

-PANNING UP, as the EXTeam looks back and noticed the blast from afar. Henry holds his head knowing that Red Falcon has killed himself to save them.

HENRY BLADES-(MICHEAL's childhood friend)

"He was a good soldier, hard-headed but he risked his life to save us."

DOCUMENTED FILE# 0000276

MICHEAL

"HENRY LOOK OUT"

125. EXT. COURTYARD - PLANET X FACILITY - NIGHT

-CAMERA TRACKS, on Henry walking directly in front of a Planet X-Tracker getting cocooned with the hardening gel. The tracker picks his body up and brings him back in the Facility in a fast pace.

(CUT TO:)

126. INT. HALLWAY - PLANET X FACILITY - NIGHT

-ANGLE, on The President looking for

DOCUMENTED FILE# 0000277

Jennifer calling her name. He calls off all of the Trackers and Gunners and speaks through his PA system outside of the facility courtyard.

(CUT TO:)

127. EXT. COURTYARD - PLANET X FACILITY - NIGHT

THE PRESIDENT OF THE UNITED STATES

[Audio Voice]

"Attention Planet X Shoppers,

this is your President speaking.

I am waiting on you so

If you want to kill me,

you will have to find me first

before I set the detonators

DOCUMENTED FILE# 0000278

on earth. You will have
the choice between saving
Jennifer or Earth.
The time is ticking,
by the way, My X-Trackers
has already made your
friends a nice Picasso on
my wall, how much can
I sell this art for? hmm…"

-HIGH WIDE ANGLE, as the PA system bleeps off. MICHEAL looks at Natasha and points to her to run to the Westside of the facility while he is running to the Eastside entrance.

MICHEAL

"Go save Henry and meet me at the

portal. I will get Jennifer and stop

the President."

NATASHA-CYBERNETIC ROBOT/EXT TEAM

"Roger that, good luck Micheal"

(CUT TO:)

**128. EXT. WESTSIDE ENTRANCE - PLANET X
FACILITY - NIGHT**

-JUMP CUT, on Natasha reaching the Westside
entrance setting a bomb on the doorway.
CLOSE-UP, on the bomb detonating blowing
the hatch.

DOCUMENTED FILE# 0000280

(CUT TO:)

129. INT. WESTSIDE ENTRANCE HALL - PLANET X FACILITY - NIGHT

-LOW WIDE ANGLE, on 4 soldiers waiting on her around the corner of a wall at the end of the hallway.

(CUT TO:)

130. INT. WESTSIDE ENTRANCE - PLANET X FACILITY - NIGHT

-WHIP PANNING, on Natasha diving into the hallways, sliding her swords from around her back. 4 guards jump out from behind

the wall. Natasha slices them up in half before they can pull the trigger their guns. TIGHT ON, Natasha doing a triple back flips into the aircraft hangar.

(CUT TO:)

131. INT. AIRCRAFT HANGER - PLANET X FACILITY - NIGHT

-ANGLE BETWEEN TWO AIRCRAFTS, on Natasha standing in the middle of the hanger. She notices that there are 4 X-Trackers and 2 mobile gunners aiming their guns towards her exact location.

-TIGHT ON, Natasha smiling. WHIP PANNING, on her shooting the gas tank of one of the aircrafts near the 2 gunners take them

both out. TIGHT ON, the aircraft debris blowing up with its metal parts splashing all over the wall behind it.

-FULL WIDE SHOT, on the X-Trackers shooting there hardening gel towards her. She jumps out of the way cart wheeling towards the left. Then looks left and notices the crate that she was standing behind before is melting to the floor.

NATASHA-CYBERNETIC ROBOT/EXT TEAM

(Whispering to herself)

"They must be using some type

of pure acid, it's burning through

anything that it touches I got to be

careful that was too close"

-FULL SHOT, on the X-Trackers trying to

pinpoint her location. ON-SCREEN SHOT, Natasha looking at her scanner and notices that Henry's beacon is not too far off from her location pass the direction of the trackers. TIGHT ON, Natasha loading her guns, while sneaking behind each aircraft. placing bombs on each one as she walks by. TIGHT ON, Her foot kicking a wrench that was on the floor. PANNING UP, on the X-Trackers jumping high into the air towards her location. REVERSE ANGLE, on The Trackers shooting out Small-Trackers. Each one of them starts to blow up as she is running out of harms way. ANGLE DOWN, on one of the Small-Trackers landing near her feet blowing up ripping part of her sleeve and pants leg. Natasha begins to slide under an aircraft yelling out to get all of the trackers attention.

NATASHA-CYBERNETIC ROBOT/EXT TEAM

(Taunting)

"Here I am, come and get me"

-FULL SHOT, on all of the X-Trackers and small-trackers following her voice. She waits for right moment and TIGHT ON, Natasha pressing the button on her device blowing up all of the bombs that's she set on the aircrafts. REVERSE ANGLE, on all the planes blowing up one by one next to the X-Trackers.

-PANNING UP, on the Two X-Trackers jumping in the air avoiding the blast and surround her. Both Trackers shoot out their acid

hardening gel but Natasha dodges out the way so fast the they shoot themselves melting each other with acid.

(CUT TO:)

132. INT. CENTRAL CORRIDOR - PLANET X FACILITY - NIGHT

-HANDHELD CAMERA, on Natasha running into a central hallway into the central corridor, where Henry's beacon is located on her scanner. REVERSE ANGLE, on Natasha detonating the last bomb, completely destroying the aircraft hanger behind her.

(CUT TO:)

133. INT. PORTAL X AREA - PLANET X FACILITY - LEVEL 2

-TIGHT ON, the President looking up as he feels the shake of the blast wondering what happened. He shrugs his head and keeps looking for Jennifer.

(CUT TO:)

134. INT. ARCHIVE ROOM - PLANET X FACILITY - LEVEL 3

-DOLLYING AHEAD, on Natasha walking out of the central corridor into the archive room where she sees Henry dangling from the wall. She climbs up the wall and rips the gel off his Henry's body. Henry falls to the floor. She take out a needle filled

DOCUMENTED FILE# 0000287

with adrenaline and pushes it into his chest. Henry wakes up abruptly wondering where he is.

HENRY BLADES-(MICHEAL's childhood friend)

"I'm still alive I thought I was dead"

[Transmission-feed break]

NATASHA-CYBERNETIC ROBOT/EXT TEAM

(Replying)

"I wasn't sure what to believe,
I guess the side effects from
the gel put you into a slight coma."

[Transmission-feed break/reboot/online]

DOCUMENTED FILE# 0000288

HENRY BLADES-(MICHEAL's childhood friend)

(Shruggish)

"Where's MICHEAL?"

NATASHA-CYBERNETIC ROBOT/EXT TEAM

"I'm not sure exactly, he entered the

Eastside entrance of the facility.

He said he was trying to

save Jennifer

and stop the President"

-TIGHT ON, Natasha picking up Henry
under her arm and starts walking to the
stairwell of the huge energy source on
level 2 beneath them.

(CUT TO:)

DOCUMENTED FILE# 0000289

135. INT. EASTSIDE ENTRANCE HALL - PLANET X FACILITY - NIGHT

-ANGLE|FOLLOW, MICHEAL walking into the hallway where the lights are completely cut off due to the President powering up the Planet X Portal. Its just about pitch black to where MICHEAL cannot see anything except for the emergency lights on the right hand side.

-CLOSE UP ON MICHEAL cocking back his gun and walking towards the Level 2 entranceway where he sees bright light. At the end of the hall.

(CUT TO:)

136. INT. PORTAL X ENTRANCE AREA|LEVEL 2

DOCUMENTED FILE# 0000290

- PLANET X FACILITY

-ON-SCREEN SHOT, of MICHEAL looking at his body scanner, noticing that there are 2 heat signals inside of the room. MICHEAL takes a deep breath and moves around the room with a firm pace. ANGLE, on MICHEAL sliding behind a wall divider and spots. The President setting up the sequence for the bomb, while activating a the instrumentation the portal. MICHEAL notices that there are detonators in his hand.

....

-PAN LEFT, on MICHEAL looking at Jennifer, sitting down in a chair knocked out. MICHEAL slowly moves into

the lower floor of the room behind The President raising his gun at him.

MICHEAL

"Stop it right there, Mr. President, Put your hands up now, and drop those detonators"

(CUT TO:)

137. INT. LOWER LEVEL PORTAL X AREA – LEVEL 2

-LOW WIDE SHOT, on The President looking back at MICHEAL chuckling before he begins to talk. The air in the room starts to suck the objects into the portal.

DOCUMENTED FILE# 0000292

THE PRESIDENT OF THE UNITED STATES

"MICHEAL is that you Micheal.
I am so glad you made it Micheal.
Remember when I told you where
going to make the biggest
decision of you life?
Choice one, I will
let you go back to Earth
saving it and give you the
sequence to the detonators,
because the bomb is already
on earth Micheal. Or choice two,
you can sit here with
Jennifer and watch me
destroy all human life
on the planet. So what
will it be? Save human life
on earth world? Or you

saving Jennifer killing me,

and watch the whole world die?"

(CUT TO:)

138. INT. WESTSIDE ENTRANCE - PORTAL X AREA - LEVEL 2

-REVERSE ANGLE, on Natasha and Henry reaching the Westside entrance to the Portal X Area. The President notices them both coming in and waves for them to join the party.

THE PRESIDENT OF THE UNITED STATES

"Come Join Us"

Talking to Natasha and Henry..

DOCUMENTED FILE# 0000294

THE PRESIDENT OF THE UNITED STATES

"Stand next to Jennifer and watch

history in the making.

I already told Micheal what

he has to do. Plus I have implanted

a Cranium Intel chip

in your brain. I've been tracking

all you positions Micheal.

So what are you

going to do? Do you really

think killing me and saving

is enough for every living

person on earth to die?

MICHEAL

(Bluffing)

"You implanted what?

Do you think I care about

DOCUMENTED FILE# 0000295

whatever Intel you received?

I don't care. Right now I don't care

about anyone else. Except for you.

That's why you will die tonight"

THE PRESIDENT OF THE UNITED STATES

"There only 40 seconds left Micheal,

bluffing will not save you now"

MICHEAL

(Yelling)

"Alright, I will leave,

just don't kill all of

those innocent people,

They don't deserve to die"

-LOW WIDE SHOT, of MICHEAL stepping up

next to the portal. The President hands

him a piece of paper that carries the real Deactivation codes for the bomb back in St. Louis. The agents that are left run into the room and begin pointing there guns towards the EXTeam. The President's points to them to stand down.

TIGHT ON- Micheal as pictures of people randomly inside of MICHEAL's head, moving faster and faster then stops. MICHEAL snaps out of the flashback, and before the President can enter the destination for MICHEAL to go back he grabs The President by the arm, pulling him into the portal with him. At the same time, Jennifer is waking up and noticing that President Whitaker and MICHEAL are falling into the portal.

DOCUMENTED FILE# 0000297

THE PRESIDENT OF THE UNITED STATES

(Yelling)

"Nooooooooo"

MICHEAL

(Yelling)

"Ahhhhhhh"

-PAN, on Henry, Natasha walking up to the portal in disbelief. The Planet X Agents put there guns down and walk up behind them looking into the portal. Jennifer begins to speak.

JENNIFER/Female Police Officer

"So what does this mean?

[Transmission-feed break]

DOCUMENTED FILE# 0000298

HENRY BLADES-(MICHEAL's childhood friend)

"I don't know. MICHEAL told

me a while back

in Africa, that if something

like this happened

where someone travels

through a portal without

a lock in destination,

they could be bumped

back or forth into time.

Maybe, even to another world,

I guess he was trying

to save all of us all along."

-ZOOM IN, through the portal, passing

through streak of light, noting many other

galaxies through space. Moving faster and

faster, back into the Milky Way, passing the

planets in our solar system. Approaching Earth, surrounding it. The camera travels though the Earth atmosphere all the way down to The Gateway Arch in St. Louis. The time has changed and the year is now 3040. PANNING DOWN, from a shot of the sun with so much pollution in the air that the sky is orange and brown. CLOSE-UP on a kid holding a balloon tapping his mother, so they can go up to the Arch for a visit.

(CUT TO:)

[*In the future, a thousand years later, Micheal's Intel feed comes from a young adolescent boy.]

139. EXT. GATEWAY ARCH - ST. LOUIS YEAR

DOCUMENTED FILE# 0000300

3040 - MIDDAY

YOUNG KID

"Hey mother can I

see inside the Arch"

YOUNG KID's MOTHER

"Yes son, of course we can.

Did you know back in 2020

we couldn't even see

the Gateway Arch. It was covered

by a building that the

government called

Portal X Facility.

After the President

disappeared they tore

down the building down

and re-built a replica

of the Gateway Arch like

DOCUMENTED FILE# 0000301

it used to be a

long, long time ago."

[Transmission-feed break/re/online]

YOUNG KID

(Replying)

"You mean it was covered up?"

YOUNG KID's MOTHER

"Yes dear, there were even

rumors that it led to

another world like ours.

With no pollution,

they even had gas powered

cars that they drove around."

DOCUMENTED FILE# 0000302

YOUNG KID

(Replying)

"Gas powered cars, cool!
Is that part of the reason
why we have to wear mask
all the time because
they made so much pollution?".

YOUNG KID's MOTHER

(Replying)

"Yes dear, for we have torn
down this world piece by
piece in ways I can't
even explain. The pollution
levels in the air have
reached above toxic
for us to breathe.
That is the reason

DOCUMENTED FILE# 0000303

why we have to wear
oxygen masks all of
the time, except for
inside of our buildings.
Breathing air without
a mask was a privilege
that our earlier generation
took for granted."

YOUNG KID

(Inspired)

"Well I want to become
a scientist, and discover
how to clean the air and
build our ozone layer
back up again"

DOCUMENTED FILE# 0000304

YOUNG KID's MOTHER

"Well, if you believe

it you can achieve it,

so let us look at our city

from the top of the Arch.

We can even go through

the tunnel below across

to the old cathedral too.

That was the original

plan from the architects

who designed it.

Come on, let's go inside.."

(CUT TO:)

140. INT. GATEWAY ARCH - MIDDAY

-ANGLE ON, on the young kid's mother taking

her son's hand heading into the center of the elevator. The security guard receives their tickets scanning them, as he begins pressing the key for the elevator doors to opens. They both walk into the tram car as they sit, heading up to observation area in the arch.

141. EXT. GATEWAY ARCH - MIDDAY

-PANNING UP, on the light from the elevator going to the top of arch.

END TRANSMISSION 12:42:45

CODE 2020_ 6 877984343

DOCUMENTED FILE# 0000306

REGISTRATION U.S. FILE NUMBER 557-2020 557-2020-3928

ALL DOCUMENTED INFORMATION

Approved.

S.C.
SCOTT COLLINS

[COMMANDER AND CHIEF EYES ONLY]

1065TH President of the United States of America

TOP SECRET

POST _ INTEL WRITTEN BY U.S.

GOVERNMENT OFFICER _ #39672966285

DOCUMENT STORED: DEPARTMENT OF DEFENSE

10701 Lambert International Bl,
St. Louis, MO-3040 AD

REGISTRATION NUMBER U.S. GOVERNMENT FILE NUMBER 5573928-2020

DOCUMENTED FILE# 0000307

In 3040, after much conspiracy theories of the Earth ending on 2012, St. Louis City became the capitol of America electing Scott Collins the 1046th President of the United States of America. Collins put an end to world hunger once he came into office. President Collins made sure he turned the District of Columbia into a memorial site in memory of the Ancient Civilization of the United States from the early 21st century.

America went into a major depression uproar at midnight on Dec. 19th, 2020. President Whitaker announced North America will be auctioned off to the highest bidder, except for State of Missouri, keeping St. Louis a haven for the elite. After a ferocious bidding war, one successful business magnate named Xavier Street, purchased the rest of North America changing the name to 99.97% of America's state names to the Circle District of America.

DOCUMENTED FILE# 0000309

All PortaL X Facility personal high-profile aircrafts including Air Force One, Marine One for the President have been moved from Washington D.C. to the new capitol of North America, St. Louis City, MO.

DOCUMENTED FILE# 0000310

St. Louis law enforcement officers
hand picked by the top of the Federal
and State Goverment operations.
Objective: Protect all borders
of St. Louis City, monitoring
the elite society at all times.

DOCUMENTED FILE# 0000311

IN GOD WE TRUST

www.ingramcontent.com/pod-product-compliance
Lightning Source LLC
Chambersburg PA
CBHW042134120726
47911CB00019B/3